双 语 名 著 无 障 碍 阅 读 丛 书

第 二 级

伊索寓言 （精选）

Aesop's Fables

(Selections)

［古希腊］伊索　著　　默里·廷克尔曼　绘图

李长山　陈贻彦　孙征　译

中 国 出 版 集 团

中 译 出 版 社

图书在版编目（CIP）数据

伊索寓言：精选：英汉对照/（古希腊）伊索著；李长山，陈贻彦，孙征译.—北京：中译出版社，2012.7（2016.11重印）

（双语名著无障碍阅读丛书）

ISBN 978-7-5001-3452-7

I.①伊… II.①伊… ②李… ③陈… ④孙… III.①英语—汉语—对照读物 ②寓言—作品集—古希腊 IV.①H319.4：I

中国版本图书馆CIP数据核字（2012）第149770号

出版发行 / 中译出版社

地　　址 / 北京市西城区车公庄大街甲4号物华大厦六层

电　　话 / （010）68359827，68359303（发行部）；53601537（编辑部）

邮　　编 / 100044

传　　真 / （010）68357870

电子邮箱 / book@ctph.com.cn

网　　址 / http://www.ctph.com.cn

出版策划 / 张高里　凌从严

执行策划 / 胡晓凯

责任编辑 / 胡晓凯　范祥镇

封面设计 / 潘　峰

排　　版 / 陈　彬

印　　刷 / 保定市中画美凯印刷有限公司

经　　销 / 新华书店

规　　格 / 710毫米×1000毫米　1/16

印　　张 / 15.5

字　　数 / 200千

版　　次 / 2012年7月第一版

印　　次 / 2016年11月第六次

ISBN 978-7-5001-3452-7　　　　　定价：22.00元

　　多年以来，中译出版社有限公司（原中国对外翻译出版有限公司）凭借国内一流的翻译和出版实力及资源，精心策划、出版了大批双语读物，在海内外读者中和业界内产生了良好、深远的影响，形成了自己鲜明的出版特色。

　　二十世纪八九十年代出版的英汉（汉英）对照"一百丛书"，声名远扬，成为一套最权威、最有特色且又实用的双语读物，影响了一代又一代英语学习者和中华传统文化研究者、爱好者；还有"英若诚名剧译丛""中华传统文化精粹丛书""美丽英文书系"，这些优秀的双语读物，有的畅销，有的常销不衰反复再版，有的被选为大学英语阅读教材，受到广大读者的喜爱，获得了良好的社会效益和经济效益。

　　"双语名著无障碍阅读丛书"是中译专门为中学生和英语学习者精心打造的又一品牌，是一个新的双语读物系列，具有以下特点：

　　选题创新——该系列图书是国内第一套为中小学生量身打造的双语名著读物，所选篇目均为教育部颁布的语文新课标必读书目，或为中学生以及同等文化水平的社会读者喜闻乐见的世界名著，重新编译为英汉（汉英）对照的双语读本。这些书既给青少年读者提供了成长过程中不可或缺的精神食粮，又让他们领略到原著的精髓和魅力，对他们更好地学习英文大有裨益；同时，丛书中入选的《论语》《茶馆》《家》等汉英对照读物，亦是热爱中国传统文化的中外读者所共知的经典名篇，能使读者充分享受阅读经典的无限乐趣。

无障碍阅读——中学生阅读世界文学名著的原著会遇到很多生词和文化难点。针对这一情况，我们给每一本读物原文中的较难词汇和不易理解之处都加上了注释，在内文的版式设计上也采取英汉（或汉英）对照方式，扫清了学生阅读时的障碍。

优良品质——中译双语读物多年来在读者中享有良好口碑，这得益于作者和出版者对于图书质量的不懈追求。"双语名著无障碍阅读丛书"继承了中译双语读物的优良传统——精选的篇目、优秀的译文、方便实用的注解，秉承着对每一个读者负责的精神，竭力打造精品图书。

愿这套丛书成为广大读者的良师益友，愿读者在英语学习和传统文化学习两方面都取得新的突破。

目
CONTENTS
录

一　黑仆人 ···································· 002

I　The Aethiop

二　蚂蚁和鸽子 ······························ 003

II　The Ant and the Dove

三　安德罗克勒斯 ···························· 004

III　Androcles

四　蚂蚁和蛹 ································ 006

IV　The Ant and the Chrysalis

五　蚂蚁和蚱蜢 ······························ 008

V　The Ants and the Grasshopper

六　驴和赶驴人 ······························ 009

VI　The Ass and His Driver

七　驴和他的主人 ···························· 010

VII　The Ass and His Masters

八　驴和他的影子 ···························· 012

VIII　The Ass and His Shadow

九　驴和买主 ································ 014

IX　The Ass and His Purchaser

十　驴和战马 ································ 016

X　The Ass and the Charger

一一　驴和青蛙 ······························ 017

XI　The Ass and the Frogs

一二　驴和蚱蜢 ······························ 018

XII　The Ass and the Grasshopper

目录
CONTENTS

一三　驴和马 ………………………………… 019

XIII　The Ass and the Horse

一四　驴和骡子 ……………………………… 020

XIV　The Ass and the Mule

一五　驴和狼 ………………………………… 022

XV　The Ass and the Wolf

一六　驴的脑子 ……………………………… 024

XVI　The Ass's Brains

一七　驮神像的驴 …………………………… 026

XVII　The Ass Carrying the Image

一八　驴、公鸡和狮子 ……………………… 027

XVIII　The Ass, the Cock, and the Lion

一九　驴、狐狸和狮子 ……………………… 028

XIX　The Ass, the Fox, and the Lion

二○　披着狮子皮的驴 ……………………… 029

XX　The Ass in the Lion's Skin

二一　天文学家 ……………………………… 030

XXI　The Astronomer

二二　秃子和苍蝇 …………………………… 031

XXII　The Bald Man and the Fly

二三　蝙蝠、鸟和兽 ………………………… 032

XXIII　The Bat, the Birds, and the Beasts

二四　熊和两个行人 ………………………… 034

XXIV　The Bear and the Two Travelers

目
CONTENTS
录

二五　蜜蜂和朱庇特 ………………………… 036
XXV　The Bee and Jupiter

二六　捕鸟人、山鹑和公鸡 ………………… 038
XXVI　The Birdcatcher, the Partridge, and the Cock

二七　盲人和狼崽 …………………………… 040
XXVII　The Blind Man and the Whelp

二八　吹牛的旅行者 ………………………… 041
XXVIII　The Boasting Traveler

二九　男孩和榛子 …………………………… 042
XXIX　The Boy and the Filberts

三〇　洗澡的男孩 …………………………… 043
XXX　The Boy Bathing

三一　捉蝗虫的男孩 ………………………… 044
XXXI　The Boy Hunting Locusts

三二　男孩和青蛙 …………………………… 045
XXXII　The Boys and the Frogs

三三　一捆木棒 ……………………………… 046
XXXIII　The Bundle of Sticks

三四　笼中鸟和蝙蝠 ………………………… 047
XXXIV　The Cage Bird and the Bat

三五　骆驼 …………………………………… 048
XXXV　The Camel

三六　骆驼和朱庇特 ………………………… 049
XXXVI　The Camel and Jupiter

目
CONTENTS
录

三七　猫和鸟 ……………………………………… 050

XXXVII　The Cat and the Birds

三八　猫和公鸡 …………………………………… 051

XXXVIII　The Cat and the Cock

三九　猫和维纳斯 ………………………………… 052

XXXIX　The Cat and Venus

四〇　烧炭人和漂洗工 …………………………… 053

XL　The Charcoal-Burner and the Fuller

四一　战马和磨坊主 ……………………………… 054

XLI　The Charger and the Miller

四二　公鸡和珍珠 ………………………………… 055

XLII　The Cock and the Pearl

四三　螃蟹母子 …………………………………… 056

XLIII　The Crab and Its Mother

四四　螃蟹和狐狸 ………………………………… 057

XLIV　The Crab and the Fox

四五　乌鸦和墨丘利 ……………………………… 058

XLV　The Crow and Mercury

四六　乌鸦和蛇 …………………………………… 059

XLVI　The Crow and the Serpent

四七　母鹿和狮子 ………………………………… 060

XLVII　The Doe and the Lion

四八　狗和野兔 …………………………………… 061

XLVIII　The Dog and the Hare

四九　狗和蚌 ·· 062

XLIX　The Dog and the Oyster

五〇　食槽里的狗 ······································· 063

L　The Dog in the Manger

五一　狗和倒影 ··· 064

LI　The Dog and the Shadow

五二　狗和牛皮 ··· 065

LII　The Dog and the Hides

五三　海豚、鲸鱼和鲱鱼 ···························· 066

LIII　The Dolphins, the Whales, and the Sprat

五四　鹰和捕鹰人 ····································· 067

LIV　The Eagle and His Captor

五五　鹰和箭 ··· 068

LV　The Eagle and the Arrow

五六　农夫和他的儿子 ······························· 069

LVI　The Farmer and His Sons

五七　农夫和蛇 ··· 070

LVII　The Farmer and the Snake

五八　打架的公鸡和鹰 ······························· 071

LVIII　The Fighting Cocks and the Eagle

五九　渔夫和小鱼 ····································· 072

LIX　The Fisher and the Little Fish

六〇　苍蝇和蜂蜜罐 ··································· 073

LX　The Flies and the Honey-Pot

目
CONTENTS
录

六一　苍蝇和拉车的骡子 ················· 074

LXI　　The Fly and the Draught-Mule

六二　捕鸟人和毒蛇 ····················· 075

LXII　　The Fowler and the Viper

六三　狐狸和猫 ························· 076

LXIII　　The Fox and the Cat

六四　狐狸和刺藤 ······················· 078

LXIV　　The Fox and the Bramble

六五　狐狸和山羊 ······················· 079

LXV　　The Fox and the Goat

六六　狐狸和乌鸦 ······················· 080

LXVI　　The Fox and the Crow

六七　狐狸和葡萄 ······················· 082

LXVII　　The Fox and the Grapes

六八　狐狸和豹子 ······················· 083

LXVIII　　The Fox and the Leopard

六九　狐狸和面具 ······················· 084

LXIX　　The Fox and the Mask

七〇　狐狸和猴子 ······················· 085

LXX　　The Fox and the Monkey

七一　丢了尾巴的狐狸 ··················· 086

LXXI　　The Fox Who Had Lost His Tail

七二　青蛙和井 ························· 087

LXXII　　The Frogs and the Well

目录
CONTENTS

七三　蚊子和公牛 ………………………… 088

LXXIII　The Gnat and the Bull

七四　山羊和牧羊人 ……………………… 089

LXXIV　The Goat and the Goatherd

七五　下金蛋的鹅 ………………………… 090

LXXV　The Goose with the Golden Eggs

七六　野兔和狐狸 ………………………… 091

LXXVI　The Hares and the Foxes

七七　野兔和猎狗 ………………………… 092

LXXVII　The Hare and the Hound

七八　野兔和狮子 ………………………… 093

LXXVIII　The Hares and the Lions

七九　龟兔赛跑 …………………………… 094

LXXIX　The Hare and the Tortoise

八〇　鹿和藤蔓 …………………………… 095

LXXX　The Hart and the Vine

八一　鹿和猎人 …………………………… 096

LXXXI　The Hart and the Hunter

八二　鹰、鸢和鸽子 ……………………… 098

LXXXII　The Hawk, the Kite, and the Pigeons

八三　母牛和公牛 ………………………… 099

LXXXIII　The Heifer and the Ox

八四　母鸡和金蛋 ………………………… 100

LXXXIV　The Hen and the Golden Eggs

目
CONTENTS
录

八五　赫拉克勒斯和马车夫 ‥‥‥‥‥‥‥‥‥‥ 101

LXXXV　Hercules and the Wagoner

八六　马和驴（版本一） ‥‥‥‥‥‥‥‥‥‥‥ 102

LXXXVI　The Horse and the Ass

八七　马和驴（版本二） ‥‥‥‥‥‥‥‥‥‥‥ 103

LXXXVII　The Horse and the Ass

八八　马和马夫 ‥‥‥‥‥‥‥‥‥‥‥‥‥‥ 104

LXXXVIII　The Horse and Groom

八九　马和鹿 ‥‥‥‥‥‥‥‥‥‥‥‥‥‥‥ 105

LXXXIX　The Horse and the Stag

九〇　马和骑兵 ‥‥‥‥‥‥‥‥‥‥‥‥‥‥ 106

XC　The Horse and His Rider

九一　猎人和伐木工 ‥‥‥‥‥‥‥‥‥‥‥‥ 108

XCI　The Hunter and the Woodman

九二　猎人和渔夫 ‥‥‥‥‥‥‥‥‥‥‥‥‥ 109

XCII　The Huntsman and the Fisherman

九三　马、猎人和鹿 ‥‥‥‥‥‥‥‥‥‥‥‥ 110

XCIII　The Horse, Hunter, and Stag

九四　墨丘利木像和木匠 ‥‥‥‥‥‥‥‥‥‥ 112

XCIV　The Image of Mercury and the Carpenter

九五　寒鸦和鸽子 ‥‥‥‥‥‥‥‥‥‥‥‥‥ 113

XCV　The Jackdaw and the Doves

九六　寒鸦和狐狸 ‥‥‥‥‥‥‥‥‥‥‥‥‥ 114

XCVI　The Jackdaw and the Fox

九七　松鸦和孔雀 ……………………………… 115

XCVII　The Jay and the Peacock

九八　朱庇特和猴子 ……………………………… 116

XCVIII　Jupiter and the Monkey

九九　小羊和狼 …………………………………… 117

IC　The Kid and the Wolf

一〇〇　鸢和天鹅 ………………………………… 118

C　The Kites and the Swans

一〇一　羔羊和狼 ………………………………… 119

CI　The Lamb and the Wolf

一〇二　国王的儿子与狮子的画像 …………… 120

CII　The King's Son and the Painted Lion

一〇三　农夫和蛇 ………………………………… 122

CIII　The Laborer and the Snake

一〇四　灯 ………………………………………… 124

CIV　The Lamp

一〇五　云雀葬父 ………………………………… 125

CV　The Lark Burying Her Father

一〇六　狮子和鹰 ………………………………… 126

CVI　The Lion and the Eagle

一〇七　狮子和野兔 ……………………………… 127

CVII　The Lion and the Hare

一〇八　狮子和老鼠 ……………………………… 128

CVIII　The Lion and the Mouse

目
CONTENTS
录

目 CONTENTS 录

一〇九　狮子和雕像 ……………………………… 129

CIX　　The Lion and the Statue

一一〇　狮子和三只公牛 …………………………… 130

CX　　The Lion and the Three Bulls

一一一　狮子、老鼠和狐狸 ………………………… 131

CXI　　The Lion, the Mouse, and the Fox

一一二　坠入爱河的狮子 …………………………… 132

CXII　　The Lion in Love

一一三　狮子、熊和狐狸 …………………………… 134

CXIII　　The Lion, the Bear, and the Fox

一一四　狮子、狐狸和驴 …………………………… 136

CXIV　　The Lion, the Fox, and the Ass

一一五　狮子、狐狸和野兽 ………………………… 138

CXV　　The Lion, the Fox, and the Beasts

一一六　母狮子 ……………………………………… 140

CXVI　The Lioness

一一七　小男孩和命运女神 ………………………… 141

CXVII　The Little Boy and Fortune

一一八　狮子的份额 ………………………………… 142

CXVIII　The Lion's Share

一一九　男人和两个心上人 ………………………… 144

CXIX　The Man and His Two Sweethearts

一二〇　男人和两个妻子 …………………………… 145

CXX　　The Man and His Two Wives

目
录

一二一　丢失的假鬃 ·················· 146

CXXI　The Lost Wig

一二二　男人和妻子 ·················· 148

CXXII　The Man and His Wife

一二三　人和狮子 ···················· 149

CXXIII　The Man and the Lion

一二四　男人和萨提儿 ················ 150

CXXIV　The Man and the Satyr

一二五　猴子和骆驼 ·················· 151

CXXV　The Monkey and the Camel

一二六　人和蛇 ······················ 152

CXXVI　The Man and the Serpent

一二七　猴子和猴妈妈 ················ 154

CXXVII　The Monkeys and Their Mother

一二八　大山分娩 ···················· 155

CXXVIII　The Mountain in Labor

一二九　北风和太阳 ·················· 156

CXXIX　The North Wind and the Sun

一三〇　橡树和芦苇 ·················· 157

CXXX　The Oak and the Reeds

一三一　橡树和樵夫 ·················· 158

CXXXI　The Oak and the Woodcutter

一三二　老人和死神 ·················· 159

CXXXII　The Old Man and Death

目录
CONTENTS

一三三　老妪和酒坛 ·························· 160

CXXXIII　The Old Woman and the Wine Jar

一三四　牛和青蛙 ·························· 161

CXXXIV　The Ox and the Frog

一三五　牛和车轴 ·························· 162

CXXXV　The Oxen and the Axle-Trees

一三六　牛和屠夫 ·························· 163

CXXXVI　The Oxen and the Butchers

一三七　山鹑和猎人 ·························· 164

CXXXVII　The Partridge and the Fowler

一三八　孔雀和鹤 ·························· 165

CXXXVIII　The Peacock and the Crane

一三九　孔雀和朱诺 ·························· 166

CXXXIX　The Peacock and Juno

一四〇　顽皮的驴 ·························· 167

CXL　The Playful Ass

一四一　石榴树、苹果树和荆棘 ·················· 168

CXLI　The Pomegranate, Apple-Tree, and Bramble

一四二　预言家 ·························· 169

CXLII　The Prophet

一四三　渡鸦和天鹅 ·························· 170

CXLIII　The Raven and the Swan

一四四　富人和皮匠 ·························· 171

CXLIV　The Rich Man and the Tanner

一四五　河与海 ·················· 172

CXLV　The Rivers and the Sea

一四六　玫瑰和不凋花 ·················· 173

CXLVI　The Rose and the Amaranth

一四七　蝎子和瓢虫 ·················· 174

CXLVII　The Scorpion and the Ladybug

一四八　海鸥和鸢 ·················· 175

CXLVIII　The Seagull and the Kite

一四九　海边的旅行者 ·················· 176

CXLIX　The Seaside Travelers

一五〇　蛇和鹰 ·················· 177

CL　The Serpent and the Eagle

一五一　蛇和锉刀 ·················· 178

CLI　The Serpent and the File

一五二　母山羊和胡子 ·················· 179

CLII　The She-Goats and Their Beards

一五三　牧羊人和狗 ·················· 180

CLIII　The Shepherd and the Dog

一五四　牧羊人和海 ·················· 181

CLIV　The Shepherd and the Sea

一五五　牧童和狼 ·················· 182

CLV　The Shepherd's Boy and the Wolf

一五六　病牡鹿 ·················· 184

CLVI　The Sick Stag

目
CONTENTS
录

一五七　牡鹿、狼和羊 ……………………… 185

CLVII　The Stag, the Wolf, and the Sheep

一五八　池边的牡鹿 …………………………… 186

CLVIII　The Stag at the Pool

一五九　燕子和乌鸦 …………………………… 188

CLIX　The Swallow and the Crow

一六〇　小偷和看门狗 ………………………… 189

CLX　The Thief and the Housedog

一六一　小偷和公鸡 …………………………… 190

CLXI　The Thieves and the Cock

一六二　口渴的鸽子 …………………………… 191

CLXII　The Thirsty Pigeon

一六三　画眉鸟和猎鸟人 ……………………… 192

CLXIII　The Thrush and the Fowler

一六四　乌龟和鸟 ……………………………… 193

CLXIV　The Tortoise and the Birds

一六五　乌龟和鹰 ……………………………… 194

CLXV　The Tortoise and the Eagle

一六六　旅行者和他的狗 ……………………… 196

CLXVI　The Traveler and His Dog

一六七　两个旅行者和梧桐树 ………………… 197

CLXVII　The Travelers and the Plane-Tree

一六八　树和斧子 ……………………………… 198

CLXVIII　The Trees and the Axe

目
CONTENTS
录

一六九　被俘的号兵 ···················· 199

CLXIX　The Trumpeter Taken Prisoner

一七〇　树和芦苇 ···················· 200

CLXX　The Tree and the Reed

一七一　受诸神庇护的树 ··············· 202

CLXXI　The Trees Under the Protection of the Gods

一七二　两只袋子 ···················· 204

CLXXII　The Two Bags

一七三　两只青蛙 ···················· 205

CLXXIII　The Two Frogs

一七四　两个罐子 ···················· 206

CLXXIV　The Two Pots

一七五　两个旅行者和斧子 ············· 207

CLXXV　The Two Travelers and the Axe

一七六　狐狸和狮子 ·················· 208

CLXXVI　The Vixen and the Lioness

一七七　核桃树 ····················· 209

CLXXVII　The Walnut-Tree

一七八　寡妇和她的小女仆 ············· 210

CLXXVIII　The Widow and Her Little Maidens

一七九　寡妇和羊 ···················· 211

CLXXIX　The Widow and the Sheep

一八〇　野驴和狮子 ·················· 212

CLXXX　The Wild Ass and the Lion

目录
CONTENTS

一八一　野猪和狐狸 ……………………… 213

CLXXXI　The Wild Boar and the Fox

一八二　狼和鹤 …………………………… 214

CLXXXII　The Wolf and the Crane

一八三　狼和狐狸 ………………………… 215

CLXXXIII　The Wolf and the Fox

一八四　狼和马 …………………………… 216

CLXXXIV　The Wolf and the Horse

一八五　狼和看家狗 ……………………… 217

CLXXXV　The Wolf and the Housedog

一八六　狼和小羊 ………………………… 218

CLXXXVI　The Wolf and the Kid

一八七　狼和羊 …………………………… 219

CLXXXVII　The Wolf and the Sheep

一八八　狼和小羊 ………………………… 220

CLXXXVIII　The Wolf and the Lamb

一八九　披着羊皮的狼（版本一）………… 222

CLXXXIX　The Wolf in Sheep's Clothing

一九〇　披着羊皮的狼（版本二）………… 223

CXC　The Wolf in Sheep's Clothing

一九一　狼、狐狸和猿 …………………… 224

CXCI　The Wolf, the Fox, and the Ape

一九二　妇人和她的母鸡 ………………… 225

CXCII　The Woman and Her Hen

一九三　年轻的贼和他的母亲 …………… 226

CXCIII　The Young Thief and His Mother

Aesop

一 黑仆人

有人买了个黑仆，听说他皮肤之所以黑，都因以前的主人没注意卫生，才弄得他满身污垢，乌黑乌黑的。主人信以为真，一到家，就用各种清洁方法，不停地给他洗刷。仆人冻得患了重感冒，但他的身上或脸色却丝毫没有变白。

黑的变不成白的，本色无法更改。

I The Aethiop

The **purchaser**① of a black servant was **persuaded**② that the color of his skin arose from dirt contracted through the neglect of his former masters. On bringing him home he **resorted**③ to every **means**④ of cleaning, and subjected the man to incessant **scrubbings**. ⑤ The servant caught a **severe**⑥ cold, but he never changed his color or **complexion**⑦.

What's bred in the **bone**⑧ will **stick**⑨ to the **flesh**⑩.

---

① purchaser /'pəːtʃəsə/ *n.* 买方,购买者
② persuade /pə'sweid/ *v.* 说服
③ resort /ri'zɔːt/ *v.* 采取某手段或方法
④ means /miːnz/ *n.* 方法,手段
⑤ scrubbing /'skrʌbiŋ/ *n.* 擦洗（刷去）
⑥ severe /si'viə/ *a.* 剧烈的,严重的
⑦ complexion /kəm'plekʃən/ *n.* 外观,面色
⑧ bone /bəun/ *n.* 骨,骨骼
⑨ stick /stik/ *v.* 粘贴,粘在一起
⑩ flesh /fleʃ/ *n.* 肉

二　蚂蚁和鸽子

　　蚂蚁到河边喝水解渴，不幸被水流卷走，眼看就要淹死了。一只鸽子正巧站在岸边的树上，他摘下一片树叶，丢在水里的蚂蚁旁边。蚂蚁爬上树叶，安全地漂回了岸边。没过多久，捕鸟人来到树下，将涂了粘鸟胶的树枝伸向树上的鸽子。蚂蚁看出了捕鸟人的企图，在他脚上狠狠咬了一口。捕鸟人一疼，手里的树枝掉在地上，声音惊动了鸽子，他拍拍翅膀，飞走了。

　　好心有好报。

II　The Ant and the Dove①

　　An Ant went to the bank of a river to **quench**② its **thirst**③, and being carried away by the rush of the **stream**④, was on the point of **drowning**⑤. A Dove sitting on a tree **overhanging**⑥ the water **plucked**⑦ a leaf and let it fall into the stream close to her. The Ant climbed onto it and **floated**⑧ in safety to the bank. Shortly afterwards a birdcatcher came and stood under the tree, and laid his lime-twigs for the Dove, which sat in the branches. The Ant, perceiving his design, stung him in the foot. In pain the birdcatcher threw down the **twigs**⑨, and the noise made the Dove take wing.

　　One good turn deserves another.

---

① dove /dʌv/ *n.* 鸽子　　　　　　② quench /kwentʃ/ *v.* 解渴
③ thirst /θəːst/ *n.* 渴　　　　　　④ stream /striːm/ *n.* 流，水流，人潮
⑤ drowning /'drauniŋ/ *a.* 溺水的　⑥ overhang /'əuvə'hæŋ/ *v.* 悬于……之上，悬垂，逼近
⑦ pluck /plʌk/ *v.* 摘，猛拉，拔　　⑧ float /fləut/ *v.* 飘，漂浮
⑨ twig /twig/ *n.* 小枝，嫩枝

三　安德罗克勒斯

　　有个名叫安德罗克勒斯的奴隶从主人家里逃走，跑进了森林。他在森林里徘徊，猛然看到一头狮子躺在地上，正在痛苦地呻吟。安德罗克勒斯先是转身就跑，见狮子并没有追赶，他觉得奇怪，就回过头来看个究竟。狮子见他走近，伸出爪子给他看，安德罗克勒斯看到狮子的爪子上扎了一根大刺，肿了起来，流着血，狮子痛苦不堪。安德罗克勒斯拔出了刺，帮狮子包扎好伤口。狮子很快就站了起来，像一条温顺的狗那样舔安德罗克勒斯的手。伤愈的狮子把安德罗克勒斯带回洞中，每天外出捕猎，带回肉来养活他。

　　但是没过多久，安德罗克勒斯和狮子都被抓住了。逃跑的奴隶被判决扔给饿了好几天的狮子。皇帝陛下率领全体朝臣来观看狮子吃人的场面。安德罗克勒斯被带到斗兽场的中间，过了一会儿，狮子也被放出了牢笼，咆哮着冲向那个受难的人。可是狮子刚一靠近安德罗克勒斯，立即认出了自己的朋友，他停下来，像亲昵的狗那样摇摆着尾巴，去舔他的手。皇帝见了，大吃一惊，赶忙召安德罗克勒斯前来询问原委。皇帝听了安德罗克勒斯的讲述，宽恕了这个奴隶，赐给他自由，还把狮子放归山林。

　　知恩图报是灵魂高尚的标志。

---

① escape /is'keip/ *v.* 逃脱，避开，溜走
② wander /'wɔndə/ *v.* 游荡
③ moan /məun/ *v.* 呻吟
④ groan /grəun/ *v.* 呻吟
⑤ pursue /pə'sjuː/ *v.* 追捕
⑥ paw /pɔː/ *n.* 爪子
⑦ thorn /θɔːn/ *n.* 刺，荆棘
⑧ capture /'kæptʃə/ *v.* 抓取，获得，迷住
⑨ spectacle /'spektəkl/ *n.* 值得看的东西
⑩ gratitude /'grætitjuːd/ *n.* 感谢的心情

III Androcles

A slave named Androcles once **escaped**[1] from his master and fled to the forest. As he was **wandering**[2] about there he came upon a Lion lying down **moaning**[3] and **groaning**[4]. At first he turned to flee, but finding that the Lion did not **pursue**[5] him, he turned back and went up to him. As he came near, the Lion put out his **paw**[6], which was all swollen and bleeding, and Androcles found that a huge **thorn**[7] had got into it, and was causing all the pain. He pulled out the thorn and bound up the paw of the Lion, who was soon able to rise and lick the hand of Androcles like a dog. Then the Lion took Androcles to his cave, and every day used to bring him meat from which to live.

But shortly afterwards both Androcles and the Lion were **captured**[8], and the slave was sentenced to be thrown to the Lion, after the latter had been kept without food for several days. The Emperor and all his Court came to see the **spectacle**[9], and Androcles was led out into the middle of the arena. Soon the Lion was let loose from his den, and rushed bounding and roaring towards his victim. But as soon as he came near to Androcles he recognized his friend, and fawned upon him, and licked his hands like a friendly dog. The Emperor, surprised at this, summoned Androcles to him, who told him the whole story. Whereupon the slave was pardoned and freed, and the Lion let loose to his native forest.

Gratitude[10] is the sign of noble souls.

四　蚂蚁和蛹

　　一只蚂蚁在太阳下东奔西跑，寻找食物，看到一只即将蜕变的蛹。蛹扭动尾巴，引起了蚂蚁的注意，他这才第一次意识到，原来这东西是活的。"可怜的家伙！"蚂蚁傲慢地大叫一声，"你的命运多么悲惨！我可以自由自在地东游西逛，要是我乐意的话，还可以爬上最高的那棵大树，可你关在那个壳里，最多也只能活动活动你那条难看的尾巴上的一两个关节。"蚂蚁的这番话，蛹都听在耳朵里，但没有出声。

　　过了几天，蚂蚁又经过这里，只看到一个空壳，蛹不见了。蚂蚁正在纳闷，忽觉头顶上有什么东西遮住了阳光，紧接着吹来一阵风，一对绚丽的蝴蝶翅膀出现在他面前。"仔细看看我，"蝴蝶说，"我就是你那可怜的朋友。只要你能让我留在这儿听你吹牛，你就继续夸耀你那四处走动和爬树的本领吧。"蝴蝶说完就飞到了空中，乘着夏日的清风，他越飞越高，很快就在蚂蚁的视野里消失了。

　　切不可以貌取人。

---

① ant /ænt/ *n.* 蚂蚁
② chrysalis /'krisəlis/ *n.* 蛹，茧
③ nimbly /'nimbli/ *ad.* 敏捷地，机敏地
④ disdainfully /dis'deinfuli/ *ad.* 轻蔑地
⑤ ascend /ə'send/ *v.* 上升，攀登
⑥ imprison /im'prizn/ *v.* 拘禁
⑦ scaly /'skeili/ *a.* 鳞状的
⑧ remain /ri'mein/ *v.* 保持
⑨ gorgeous /'gɔːdʒəs/ *a.* 绚丽的
⑩ deceptive /di'septiv/ *a.* 迷惑的，导致误解的

IV   The Ant① and the Chrysalis②

An Ant **nimbly**③ running about in the sunshine in search of food came across a Chrysalis that was very near its time of change. The Chrysalis moved its tail, and thus attracted the attention of the Ant, who then saw for the first time that it was alive. "Poor, pitiable animal!" cried the Ant **disdainfully**④. "What a sad fate is yours! While I can run hither and thither, at my pleasure, and, if I wish, **ascend**⑤ the tallest tree, you lie **imprisoned**⑥ here in your shell, with power only to move a joint or two of your **scaly**⑦ tail." The Chrysalis heard all this, but did not try to make any reply.

A few days after, when the Ant passed that way again, nothing but the shell **remained**⑧. Wondering what had become of its contents, he felt himself suddenly shaded and fanned by the **gorgeous**⑨ wings of a beautiful Butterfly. "Behold in me," said the Butterfly, "your much-pitied friend! Boast now of your powers to run and climb as long as you can get me to listen." So saying, the Butterfly rose in the air, and, borne along and aloft on the summer breeze, was soon lost to the sight of the Ant forever.

Appearances are **deceptive**⑩.

五　蚂蚁和蚱蜢

　　在晴朗的冬日，蚂蚁们正忙着翻晒夏天收集的粮食。一只饥饿的蚱蜢走过来，恳切地向蚂蚁讨一点吃的。蚂蚁问蚱蜢："你为什么不在夏天储存点粮食呢？"蚱蜢回答道："那时候我一直在唱歌，没工夫干活。"蚂蚁于是嘲笑蚱蜢说："你这人太蠢，整个夏天都被你唱过去了，那么到了冬天，你就该从早到晚饿着肚子跳舞吧。"

　　未雨绸缪，才能防患于未然。

V　The Ants and the Grasshopper①

The Ants were spending a fine winter's day **drying**② grain collected in the summertime. A Grasshopper, **perishing**③ with **famine**④, passed by and **earnestly**⑤ begged for a little food. The Ants **inquired**⑥ of him, "Why did you not **treasure**⑦ up food during the summer？" He replied, "I had not **leisure**⑧ enough. I passed the days in singing." They then said in **derision**⑨: "If you were **foolish**⑩ enough to sing all the summer, you must dance supperless to bed in the winter."

It is thrifty to prepare today for the wants of tomorrow.

---

① grasshopper /'grɑːʃɔpə/ *n.* 蚱蜢
② dry /drai/ *v.* 把……弄干，干掉
③ perish /'periʃ/ *v.* 毁减，死亡
④ famine /'fæmin/ *n.* 饥荒
⑤ earnestly /'əːnistli/ *ad.* 恳切地
⑥ inquire /in'kwaiə/ *v.* 询问
⑦ treasure /'treʒə/ *v.* 储藏
⑧ leisure /'leʒə; 'liːʒə/ *n.* 空闲，闲暇
⑨ derision /di'riʒən/ *n.* 嘲笑
⑩ foolish /'fuːliʃ/ *a.* 愚蠢的

六　驴和赶驴人

　　驴被赶着走在山路上，忽然间一下子窜到了陡峭的悬崖边。就在驴快要跳下山的时候，赶驴人一把揪住了驴尾巴，想用力把他拉回来。但驴拼命挣扎，赶驴人只好放手，让驴掉下山崖，他说道："挣扎吧，但结果是送了你自己的命。"

　　一意孤行的家伙总是不撞南墙不回头。

VI　The Ass and His Driver

　　An **Ass**①, being driven along a high road, suddenly **started off**② and **bolted**③ to the brink of a deep **precipice**④. While he was in the act of throwing himself over, his owner **seized**⑤ him by the tail, **endeavoring**⑥ to pull him back. When the Ass **persisted**⑦ in his effort, the man let him go and said, "**Conquer**⑧, but conquer to your cost."

　　A **willful**⑨ **beast**⑩ must go his own way.

---

① ass /æs/ n. 驴,愚蠢的人,臀部
② start off v. 出发（动身,开始）
③ bolt /bəult/ v. 冲出去,急逃
④ precipice /'presipis/ n. 断崖,绝壁
⑤ seize /si:z/ v. 抓住
⑥ endeavor /in'devə/ v. 努力,尽力
⑦ persist /pə'sist/ v. 坚持
⑧ conquer /'kɔŋkə/ v. 克服,征服,战胜
⑨ willful /'wilful/ a. 任性的,倔强的
⑩ beast /bi:st/ n. 畜生

七　驴和他的主人

　　有头驴给草药贩子干活，食物少，活又重，他就求朱庇特不要让他再干现在的活了，给他另换一个主人。朱庇特警告驴说，他会为这个请求后悔的，然后就设法把驴卖给了一个制瓦工。驴来到砖场后不久就发觉，自己拉的车更沉了，活也更重了，于是他又求朱庇特给他再换个主人。朱庇特告诉驴，这是他最后一次答应驴的请求，然后就命令把驴卖给了一个皮匠。驴见到了主人的工作，不禁哀叹自己命运不济："我宁愿在原来的主人那里挨饿，或是为另一个主人受累，也强过被现在这个主人买来，他在我死后也不会放过我，还要剥我的皮。"

　　有的人在一处不满意，在别处也难得顺心。

VII The Ass and His Masters

An Ass, **belonging to**① an herb-seller who gave him too little food and too much work made a **petition**② to **Jupiter**④ to be **released**④ from his present service and provided with another master. Jupiter, after warning him that he would repent his request, caused him to be sold to a **tile-maker**⑤. Shortly afterwards, finding that he had heavier loads to carry and harder work in the brick-field, he petitioned for another change of master. Jupiter, telling him that it would be the last time that he could **grant**⑥ his request, **ordained**⑦ that he be sold to a tanner. The Ass found that he had fallen into worse hands, and noting his master's **occupation**⑧, said, groaning: "It would have been better for me to have been either starved by the one, or to have been **overworked**⑨ by the other of my former masters, than to have been bought by my present owner, who will even after I am dead **tan**⑩ my **hide**⑪, and make me useful to him."

He that finds **discontentment**⑫ in one place is not likely to find happiness in another.

---

① belong to *v.* 属于

② petition /pi'tiʃən/ *n.* 祈求,祈祷

③ Jupiter /'dʒuːpitə/ *n.* 朱庇特

④ release /ri'liːs/ *v.* 释放

⑤ tile /tail/ *n.* 砖瓦

⑥ grant /graːnt/ *v.* 同意

⑦ ordain /ɔː'dein/ *v.* 命令

⑧ occupation /ˌɔkju'peiʃən/ *n.* 职业

⑨ overwork /'əuvə'wəːk/ *v.* 过度工作

⑩ tan /tæn/ *v.* 鞣 (革);硝 (皮)

⑪ hide /haid/ *n.* 兽皮

⑫ discontentment /ˌdiskən'tentmənt/ *n.* 不满

八　驴和他的影子

　　有个旅行者要出远门，雇了一头驴作为坐骑。天气非常热，强烈的阳光炙烤着大地。旅行者停下来休息，在驴的影子底下躲阴凉。但是影子的面积太小，只容得下一个人，旅行者和驴的主人都想享受这片阴凉，两人激烈地争吵起来。驴的主人说，他只出租驴，不出租驴的影子。旅行者说，自己既然雇了驴，自然也就连驴的影子一起雇下了。争吵很快就发展成了厮打。正当两人打得不可开交的时候，驴一溜烟地跑掉了。

　　为了影子而争吵往往会连实物一起丢掉。

VIII The Ass and His Shadow①

A Traveler **hired**② an Ass to **convey**③ him to a distant place. The day being **intensely**④ hot, and the sun shining in its strength, the Traveler stopped to rest, and sought shelter from the heat under the Shadow of the Ass. As this **afforded**⑤ only **protection**⑥ for one, and as the Traveler and the owner of the Ass both claimed it, a violent dispute arose between them as to which of them had the right to the Shadow. The owner maintained that he had let the Ass only, and not his Shadow. The Traveler **asserted**⑦ that he had, with the hire of the Ass, hired his Shadow also. The quarrel **proceeded**⑧ from words to **blows**⑨, and while the men fought, the Ass **galloped**⑩ off.

In quarreling about the shadow we often lose the substance.

---

① shadow /'ʃædəu/ *n.* 影子
② hire /'haiə/ *v.* 租用
③ convey /kən'vei/ *v.* 运输,转移
④ intensely /in'tensli/ *ad.* 强烈地
⑤ afford /ə'fɔːd/ *v.* 提供
⑥ protection /prə'tekʃən/ *n.* 保护
⑦ assert /ə'səːt/ *v.* 主张,断言
⑧ proceed /prə'siːd/ *v.* 继续进行
⑨ blow /bləu/ *n.* 重击
⑩ gallop /'gæləp/ *v.* 飞驰,急速进行

九　驴和买主

有个人到市场上去买驴，看到一头长相很漂亮的驴，就同驴的主人商量好，同意他先把他牵回家去试试看。到家以后，这人把驴关在牲口棚里，让他同其他驴待在一起。新来的驴四处看了看，立刻跑过去站在一头最好吃懒做的驴旁边。

那人看到这种情景，立刻给驴拴上了缰绳，牵回去还给了他原来的主人。驴的主人看到他这么快就回来，感到非常奇怪，就问道："你这么快就试出驴的秉性了吗?"那人答道："我不需要再试了，看他为自己选什么朋友，就知道他的本性如何。"

看一个人结交的朋友，就可了解此人的品行。

IX　The Ass and His Purchaser

A Man who wanted to buy an Ass went to **market**①, and, coming across a likely-looking beast, **arranged with**② the owner that he should be **allowed**③ to take him home on **trial**④ to see what he was like. When he reached home, he put him into his **stable**⑤ along with the other asses. The **newcomer**⑥ took a look round, and **immediately**⑦ went and chose a place next to the **laziest**⑧ and **greediest**⑨ beast in the stable.

When the master saw this he put a **halter**⑩ on him at once, and led him off and handed him over to his owner again. The latter was a good deal surprised to see him back so soon, and said, "Why, do you mean to say you have tested him already?" "I don't want to put him through any more tests," replied the other. "I could see what sort of beast he is from the companion he chose for himself."

A man is known by the company he keeps.

---

① market /ˈmɑːkit/ n. 市场
② arrange with 约定,商定
③ allow /əˈlau/ v. 允许,准许
④ trial /ˈtraiəl/ n. 尝试
⑤ stable /ˈsteibl/ n. 马厩
⑥ newcomer /ˈnjuːkʌmə/ n. 新来的人
⑦ immediately /iˈmiːdjətli/ ad. 立即
⑧ laziest /ˈleizist/ a. 最懒惰的
⑨ greediest /ˈɡriːdist/ a. 最贪婪的
⑩ halter /ˈhɔːltə/ n. 缰绳

十　驴和战马

驴羡慕战马的饲料丰富，又能得到精心的照料，而自己的草料一向不足，还要干重活。战争爆发了，全副武装的士兵跨上战马，骑着他冲锋陷阵，同敌人短兵相接。战马遍体鳞伤，死在了战场上。驴看到马的遭遇，改变了以前的想法，反倒同情起战马来了。

X　The Ass and the Charger①

An Ass **congratulated**② a Horse on being so **ungrudgingly**③ and carefully provided for, while he himself had **scarcely**④ enough to eat and not even that without hard work. But when war broke out, a heavily armed soldier **mounted**⑤ the Horse, and **riding**⑥ him to the charge, rushed into the very **midst**⑦ of the enemy. The Horse was **wounded**⑧ and fell dead on the **battlefield**⑨. Then the Ass, seeing all these things, changed his mind, and **commiserated**⑩ the Horse.

---

① charger /'tʃɑːdʒə/ *n.* 军马
② congratulate /kən'grætjuleit/ *v.* 祝贺
③ ungrudgingly /'ʌn'grʌdʒiŋli/ *a.* 慷慨地,情愿地
④ scarcely /'skɛəsli/ *ad.* 几乎不,简直没有
⑤ mount /maunt/ *v.*骑上马
⑥ ride /raid/ *v.* 骑
⑦ midst /'midst/ *n.* 中间,当中
⑧ wound /wuːnd/ *v.* 伤害
⑨ battlefield /'bætlfiːld/ *n.* 战场
⑩ commiserate /kə'mizəreit/ *v.* 怜悯,同情

一一 驴和青蛙

有头驴驮着木料过池塘，不小心失足摔倒了，背上驮的东西太沉，压得他站不起来，于是驴便大声呻吟起来。在池塘里来来往往的青蛙听到了驴的哀叹，说道："你只不过一跤摔在水里，就这样长吁短叹，要是你像我们这样在此长住，又该怎么办呢？"

人可以在巨大的不幸面前表现得很勇敢，但一次小小的挫折却足以让他丧胆。

XI The Ass and the Frogs①

An Ass, carrying a load of wood, passed through a pond. As he was crossing through the water he lost his footing, **stumbled**② and fell, and not being able to rise **on account of**③ his load, groaned heavily. Some Frogs **frequenting**④ the pool heard his **lamentation**⑤, and said, "What would you do if you had to live here always as we do, when you make such a **fuss**⑥ about a **mere**⑦ fall into the water?"

Men often bear little **grievances**⑧ with less **courage**⑨ than they do large **misfortunes**⑩.

---

① frog /frɔg/ n. 蛙
② stumble /'stʌmbl/ v. 绊脚
③ on account of 因为，由于
④ frequent /'friːkwənt/ v. 常到，常去
⑤ lamentation /ˌlæmen'teiʃən/ n. 悲痛，哀悼，痛哭
⑥ fuss /fʌs/ n. 大惊小怪，小题大做
⑦ mere /miə/ a. 仅仅的，只不过
⑧ grievance /'griːvəns/ n. 委屈，冤情，苦况
⑨ courage /'kʌridʒ/ n. 勇气
⑩ misfortune /mis'fɔːtʃən/ n. 不幸，灾祸

一二 驴和蚱蜢

驴听见蚱蜢唱歌，被他们美妙的歌声迷住了，也想唱出这样悦耳的旋律，就问蚱蜢：“你们吃了什么，才有如此美妙的歌喉？”蚱蜢回答道：“露水。”于是驴决定从此以后只喝露水，但不久便饿死了。

傻瓜也有明白的时候，只是为时太晚。

XII   The Ass and the Grasshopper

An Ass having heard some Grasshoppers **chirping**①, was highly **enchanted**②; and, desiring to **possess**③ the same charms of **melody**④, demanded what sort of food they lived on to give them such beautiful voices. They replied, "The **dew**⑤." The Ass **resolved**⑥ that he would live only upon dew, and in a short time died of hunger.

Even a fool is wise—when it is too late!

---

① chirp /tʃəːp/ *n.* 喳喳声, 唧唧声
② enchant /inˈtʃɑːnt/ *v.* 使(某人)陶醉
③ possess /pəˈzes/ *v.* 具有(某品质)
④ melody /ˈmelədi/ *n.* 旋律, 曲子, 美的音乐, 曲调
⑤ dew /djuː/ *n.* 露水
⑥ resolve /riˈzɔlv/ *v.* 决定, 决心

一三　驴和马

驴请求马把他的食物分给自己一点，马说道："可以。看在我又高贵又体面的份上，我可以把此刻吃剩下的草料都给你，如果有草料剩下的话。如果你晚上到我的马厩来，我可以给你满满一小袋大麦。"驴听了，答道："谢了，但你现在连一点点草都不肯分给我，将来又怎么肯给我更好的东西呢？"

XIII　The Ass and the Horse

An Ass **besought**[1] a Horse to spare him a small **portion**[2] of his feed. "Yes," said the Horse, "if any remains out of what I am now eating I will give it to you for the sake of my own **superior**[3] **dignity**[4], and if you will come when I reach my own **stall**[5] in the evening, I will give you a little **sack**[6] full of **barley**[7]." The Ass replied, "Thank you. But I can't think that you, who refuse me a little matter now, will by and by **confer**[8] on me a greater benefit."

---

① besought /bi'sɔːt/ v.（beseech的过去式）恳求
② portion /'pɔːʃən/ n. 部分
③ superior /sjuː'piəriə/ a. 上好的，出众的
④ dignity /'digniti/ n. 尊严
⑤ stall /stɔːl/ n. 牲畜棚中的一栏
⑥ sack /sæk/ n. 袋子
⑦ barley /'bɑːli/ n. 大麦
⑧ confer /kən'fəː/ v. 赠予

一四　驴和骡子

有个赶骡子的人赶着一头驴和一头骡子上路，他们背上都驮着沉甸甸的货物。驴在平地上走得很轻松，但一登上陡峭的山路，驴就驮不动了。驴请骡子帮他分担一小部分货物，好让自己能驮着其余的货继续赶路。但骡子对驴的话置之不理。没一会工夫，驴在重负之下从山上滚了下去，摔死了。在荒郊野外，赶骡人没有别的办法，只好把驴驮的货物也放到了骡子的背上，而且还在上面加上了一张剥下来的驴皮。骡子被压的气喘吁吁，自言自语道："我真是活该！假如在驴需要时我乐意帮他一把，现在就不会既驮着他的货物，又驮着他的皮了。"

一分预防胜过十分补救。

XIV　The Ass and the Mule

A Muleteer set forth on a journey, driving before him an Ass and a Mule, both well laden. The Ass, as long as he traveled along the **plain**①, carded his load with ease, but when he began to **ascend**② the steep path of the **mountain**③, felt his load to be more than he could bear. He **entreated**④ his **companion**⑤ to **relieve**⑥ him of a small portion, that he might carry home the rest; but the Mule **paid no attention**⑦ to the request. The Ass shortly afterwards fell down dead under his burden. Not knowing what else to do in so wild a **region**⑧, the Muleteer placed upon the Mule the load carded by the Ass in addition to his own, and at the top of all placed the hide of the Ass, after he had skinned him. The Mule, groaning **beneath**⑨ his heavy burden, said to himself. "I am treated according to my deserts. If I had only been willing to assist the Ass a little in his need, I should not now be bearing, together with his burden, himself as well."

An **ounce**⑩ of prevention is worth a pound of cure.

---

① plain /plein/ *n.* 平原
② ascend /ə'send/ *v.* 攀登
③ mountain /'mauntin/ *n.* 山
④ entreat /in'triːt/ *v.* 恳求,乞求
⑤ companion /kəm'pænjən/ *n.* 同伴
⑥ relieve /ri'liːv/ *v.* 减轻
⑦ pay attention to 注意
⑧ region /'riːdʒən/ *n.* 地区,地域,地带
⑨ beneath /bi'niːθ/ *prep.* 在……之下
⑩ ounce /auns/ *n.* 盎司

一五　驴和狼

　　驴在草地上吃草，看见狼向他冲过来，就立刻装出瘸腿的样子。狼来到驴面前，问他是怎么瘸的，驴说是过篱笆的时候，脚上扎了一根尖刺。驴劝狼帮他把刺拔出来，免得吃他的时候被刺卡住喉咙。狼信以为真，便抓起了驴腿，仔仔细细地找那根刺。驴趁机用脚对准狼的嘴，用力一踢，踢掉了狼的牙齿，然后飞快地逃走了。狼吃足了苦头，说道："这叫自作自受。老爸只教我当屠夫，我为什么偏要改行行医呢？"

XV　The Ass and the Wolf

An Ass feeding in a **meadow**① saw a Wolf **approaching**② to seize him, and immediately pretended to be **lame**③. The Wolf, coming up, inquired the cause of his lameness. The Ass replied that passing through a **hedge**④ he had trod with his foot upon a sharp thorn. He requested that the Wolf pull it out, **lest**⑤ when he ate him it should injure his **throat**⑥. The Wolf **consented**⑦ and lifted up the foot, and was giving his whole mind to the discovery of the thorn, when the Ass, with his **heels**⑧, kicked his teeth into his mouth and galloped away. The Wolf, being thus fearfully **mauled**⑨, said, "I am rightly served, for why did I attempt the art of healing, when my father only taught me the trade of a **butcher**⑩?"

---

① meadow /'medəu/ n. 草地,牧场
② approach /ə'prəutʃ/ v. 靠近,接近
③ lame /leim/ a. 跛足的
④ hedge /hedʒ/ n. 树篱
⑤ lest /lest/ conj. 以免
⑥ throat /θrəut/ n. 喉咙
⑦ consent /kən'sent/ v. 同意
⑧ heel /hiːl/ n. 脚后跟
⑨ maul /mɔːl/ v. 打伤
⑩ butcher /'butʃə/ n. 屠夫

一六　驴的脑子

　　狮子和狐狸一起外出打猎。狮子听了狐狸的主意，送信给驴，表示希望两家结成盟友。驴兴冲冲地来到约会地点，一路上幻想着和狮子的神圣同盟。但是驴刚一露面，狮子就扑过来抓住了他，然后对狐狸说："这是我们今天的晚饭。你在这儿看着他，我去睡一会儿。如果你敢碰一下我的食物，你就会倒大霉！"狮子走了，留下狐狸独自看守着驴。狐狸趁狮子不在，偷偷把驴的脑子取出来吃掉了。狮子回来时很快就发现驴的脑子不见了，于是恶狠狠地问狐狸："你把驴的脑子弄到哪去了？""驴的脑子？大王，驴根本就没脑子，要不然，他怎么会中了您的圈套呢？"

　　聪明人总能找到现成的答案。

XVI The Ass's Brains

The **Lion**[1] and the Fox went **hunting**[2] together. The Lion, on the advice of the Fox, sent a **message**[3] to the Ass, proposing to make an **alliance**[4] between their two families. The Ass came to the place of meeting, **overjoyed**[5] at the prospect of a **royal**[6] alliance. But when he came there the Lion simply **pounced**[7] on the Ass, and said to the Fox: "Here is our dinner for today. Watch you here while I go and have a nap. Woe **betide**[8] you if you touch my prey." The Lion went away and the Fox waited; but finding that his master did not return, ventured to take out the brains of the Ass and ate them up. When the Lion came back he soon noticed the absence of the brains, and asked the Fox in a terrible voice: "What have you done with the brains? " "Brains, your **Majesty**[9]! it had none, or it would never have fallen into your trap."

Wit[10] has always an answer ready.

① lion /'laiən/ n. 狮子
② hunt /hʌnt/ v. 狩猎，打猎
③ message /'mesidʒ/ n. 消息，信息
④ alliance /ə'laiəns/ n. 结盟，联盟
⑤ overjoyed /ˌəuvə'dʒɔid/ a. 极高兴
⑥ royal /'rɔiəl/ a. 王室的，皇家的
⑦ pounce /pauns/ v. 猛扑
⑧ betide /bi'taid/ v. 发生于
⑨ majesty /'mædʒisti/ n. 陛下
⑩ wit /wit/ n. 智力，才智

一七　驮神像的驴

一头驴驮着一尊有名的木神像，被人赶着在城里穿街过巷，到神庙去安置神像。路上的行人都对神像顶礼膜拜，驴以为大家是在拜他，就趾高气扬地摆起了架子，再也不肯向前走一步。赶驴人看驴停在原地不动，就用鞭子在驴背上一顿猛抽，骂道："蠢东西，人们拜驴的时候还早着呢！"

借别人的荣耀来吹嘘自己是不明智的。

XVII　The Ass Carrying the Image

An Ass once carried through the streets of a city a famous wooden Image, to be placed in one of its Temples. As he passed along, the **crowd**① made lowly **prostration**② before the Image. The Ass, thinking that they **bowed**③ their heads in **token**④ of respect for himself, **bristled**⑤ up with pride, gave himself airs, and refused to move another step. The driver, seeing him thus stop, laid his **whip**⑥ **lustily**⑦ about his shoulders and said, "O you **perverse**⑧ dull-head! It is not yet come to this, that men pay **worship**⑨ to an Ass."

They are not wise who give to themselves the **credit**⑩ due to others.

---

① crowd /kraud/ *n.* 人群　　　　　② prostration /prɔs'treiʃən/ *n.* 平伏，跪倒
③ bow /bəu/ *v.* 鞠躬，弯腰　　　　④ token /'təukən/ *n.* 表征
⑤ bristle /'brisl/ *v.* (动物的毛)竖起　⑥ whip /(h)wip/ *n.* 鞭
⑦ lustily /'lʌstili/ *ad.* 精力充沛地，强壮地　⑧ perverse /pə'vɔːs/ *a.* 乖张的，倔强的
⑨ worship /'wəːʃip/ *n.* 崇拜　　　　⑩ credit /'kredit/ *n.* 荣誉

一八 驴、公鸡和狮子

驴和公鸡一起在围栏里，忽然来了一只饥肠辘辘的狮子，正当狮子就要扑向驴的时候，公鸡放声大叫，狮子听了，掉头就跑。据说狮子非常害怕听到公鸡的叫声。驴看到公鸡的叫声都可以吓走狮子，勇气大振，跟在狮子后面紧追不舍，要给狮子一个教训。可是驴才追了没多远，狮子忽然转过身来，一把抓住驴，把他撕成了碎片。

愚蠢的自信往往招致危险。

XVIII The Ass, the Cock, and the Lion

An Ass and a Cock were in a straw yard together when a Lion, **desperate**① from hunger, approached the **spot**②. He **was about to**③ **spring**④ upon the Ass, when the Cock (to the sound of whose voice the Lion, it is said, has a **singular**⑤ **aversion**⑥) crowed loudly, and the Lion fled away as fast as he could. The Ass, observing his **trepidation**⑦ at the mere crowing of a Cock **summoned**⑧ courage to attack him, and **galloped**⑨ after him for that purpose. He had run no long distance, when the Lion, turning about, seized him and **tore**⑩ him to pieces.

False confidence often leads into danger.

---

① desperate /'despərit/ *a.* 不顾一切的,绝望的
② spot /spɒt/ *n.* 地点
③ be about to 即将
④ spring /sprɪŋ/ *v.* 弹起,跳
⑤ singular /'sɪŋgjulə/ *a.* 独一的
⑥ aversion /ə'vɔːʃən/ *n.* 嫌恶,憎恨
⑦ trepidation /trepi'deiʃən/ *n.* 恐惧,惊惶
⑧ summon /'sʌmən/ *v.* 出发,挥出
⑨ gallop /'gæləp/ *n.* 恐惧,惊惶
⑩ tore /tɔː/ *v.* 撕破

一九　驴、狐狸和狮子

　　驴和狐狸结伴去森林中打猎，相约互相保护。他们没走多远就碰到了狮子。狐狸见大难临头，就跑到狮子面前，答应想办法把驴抓到交给他，只要狮子能保证不吃他。于是，狐狸就去把驴引进了一个很深的陷阱，还告诉驴说这样很安全。狮子见驴跑不掉了，就一把捉住了狐狸，然后又轻松地把驴也抓住了。

　　千万不要相信你的敌人。

XIX　The Ass, the Fox, and the Lion

　　The Ass and the Fox, having entered into **partnership**① together for their **mutual**② protection, went out into the forest to hunt. They had not proceeded far when they met a Lion. The Fox, seeing **imminent**③ **danger**④, approached the Lion and promised to **contrive**⑤ for him the capture of the Ass if the Lion would **pledge**⑥ his word not to harm the Fox. Then, upon assuring the Ass that he would not be injured, the Fox led him to a deep **pit**⑦ and arranged that he should fall into it. The Lion, seeing that the Ass was secured, immediately **clutched**⑧ the Fox, and **attacked**⑨ the Ass at his leisure.

　　Never trust your enemy.

---

① partnership /ˈpɑːtnəʃip/ *n.* 合伙　　　　② mutual /ˈmjuːtjuəl/ *a.* 共同的，相互的
③ imminent /ˈiminənt/ *a.* 逼近的，即将发生的　　④ danger /ˈdeindʒə/ *n.* 危险
⑤ contrive /kənˈtraiv/ *v.* 设计，图谋　　⑥ pledge /pledʒ/ *v.* 保证，誓言
⑦ pit /pit/ *n.* 深坑　　　　　　　　　　⑧ clutch /klʌtʃ/ *v.* 抓牢
⑨ attack /əˈtæk/ *v.* 攻击

二〇 披着狮子皮的驴

猎人把一张狮子皮晒在外面，驴看见了，就把狮子皮披在身上，朝自己的村庄走去。村民和牲口看见驴走过来，吓得纷纷逃走。驴十分得意，高兴得扯开嗓门大叫起来，可是他刚一开口，人人都知道他不过是一头驴，受了惊的驴主人用木棒将驴暴打了一顿。随后，一只狐狸凑过来对驴说："啊，我一听声音就知道是你。"

漂亮的衣服可以掩饰傻瓜，但蠢话会暴露天性。

XX The Ass in the Lion's Skin

An Ass once found a Lion's skin which the **hunters**① had left out in the sun to dry. He put it on and went towards his native village. All fled at his approach, both men and animals, and he was a proud Ass that day. In his **delight**② he **lifted up**③ his voice and **brayed**④, but then every one knew him, and his owner came up and gave him a sound **cudgeling**⑤ for the **fright**⑥ he had caused. And shortly afterwards a Fox came up to him and said: "Ah, I knew you by your voice."

Fine clothes may **disguise**⑦, but silly words will **disclose**⑧ a fool.

---

① hunter /'hʌntə/ *n.* 猎人
② delight /di'lait/ *n.* 快乐，高兴
③ lift up 鼓舞，激励
④ bray /brei/ *v.* （驴）叫
⑤ cudgel /'kʌdʒəl/ *v.* 用棍棒打
⑥ fright /frait/ *n.* 惊骇，吃惊
⑦ disguise /dis'gaiz/ *v.* 隐藏，遮掩
⑧ disclose /dis'kləuz/ *v.* 揭露

二一　天文学家

　　有个天文学家，每天晚上都到外面去观测星象。有一天晚上，天文学家来到野外，全神贯注望着星空，不留神跌进了一口深井，身上碰得青一块、紫一块。他一面呻吟，一面大声呼救。他的邻居跑来问明原委，对他说道："老朋友，你一心只想着天上，为什么不肯分神看看地上的事？"

XXI　The Astronomer①

An Astronomer used to go out at night to observe the stars. one evening, as he **wandered**② through the **suburbs**③ with his whole attention **fixed on**④ the sky, he fell accidentally into a deep **well**⑤. While he **lamented**⑥ and **bewailed**⑦ his **sores**⑧ and **bruises**⑨, and cried loudly for help, a neighbor ran to the well, and learning what had happened said: "Hark ye, old fellow, why, in striving to **pry into**⑩ what is in heaven, do you not manage to see what is on earth？"

---

① astronomer /ə'strɔnəmə/ *n.* 天文学家
② wander /'wɔndə/ *v.* 游荡
③ suburb /'sʌbəːb/ *n.* 郊区
④ fix on 固定
⑤ well /wel/ *n.* 井
⑥ lament /lə'ment/ *v.* 悲叹
⑦ bewail /bi'weil/ *v.* 痛哭
⑧ sore /sɔː/ *n.* 痛处，疮口
⑨ bruise /bruːz/ *n.* 瘀伤，擦伤
⑩ pry into 探问

二二 秃子和苍蝇

一只苍蝇叮了秃子的头，秃子想打死苍蝇，却给了自己狠狠一巴掌。逃走的苍蝇幸灾乐祸地说："被一只小虫子叮了一下，你就要报复，甚至还想杀了这只小虫，可到头来居然又挨打又丢面子。"秃子答道："我打自己两下有什么要紧？因为我不会存心伤害自己。可是你这只可恨、无耻的小虫子，专靠吸人血取乐，我真希望一下子拍死你，就算吃再大的苦头我也不在乎!"

报复别人的人自己也会受苦。

XXII The Bald Man and the Fly

A Fly bit the bare head of a **Bald**① Man who, endeavoring to destroy it, gave himself a heavy **slap**②. Escaping, the Fly said **mockingly**③, "You who have wished to **revenge**④, even with death, the **prick**⑤ of a tiny **insect**⑥, see what you have done to yourself to add **insult**⑦ to **injury**⑧? " The Bald Man replied, "I can easily make peace with myself, because I know there was no intention to hurt. But you, an ill-favored and contemptible insect who delights in sucking human blood, I wish that I could have killed you even if I had incurred a heavier **penalty**⑨."

Revenge will hurt the **avenger**⑩.

---

① bald /bɔːld/ *a.* 秃头的　　　　　② slap /slæp/ *n.* 掴
③ mockingly /ˈmɔkiŋli/ *ad.* 愚弄地，取笑地　④ revenge /riˈvendʒ/ *v.* 报仇，报复
⑤ prick /prik/ *v.* 刺，穿　　　　　⑥ insect /ˈinsekt/ *n.* 昆虫
⑦ insult /ˈinsʌlt/ *n.* 侮辱　　　　⑧ injury /ˈindʒəri/ *n.* 损害，伤害
⑨ penalty /ˈpenlti/ *n.* 处罚，惩罚　⑩ avenger /əˈvendʒə/ *n.* 复仇者

二三　蝙蝠、鸟和兽

鸟类和兽类之间即将爆发一场大战。当双方各自集合军队的时候，蝙蝠不知道自己该加入哪一边。鸟们飞过蝙蝠的家门，对他说："来和我们并肩战斗吧。"蝙蝠答道："我是一只兽。"兽们从树下经过，抬头对蝙蝠说："来和我们并肩战斗吧。"蝙蝠答道："我是一只鸟。"幸好鸟兽双方在最后时刻和解了，没有出现战争。于是蝙蝠飞到鸟群里，想同大家一起庆贺，可所有的鸟都不理他。蝙蝠只好飞到兽群中，但没过一会儿，蝙蝠就落荒而逃，不然的话，那些野兽非把他撕成碎片不可。蝙蝠叹道："唉，我现在才明白，没有立场的人是找不到朋友的。"

XXIII   The Bat, the Birds, and the Beasts

A great **conflict**[①] was about to come off between the Birds and the Beasts. When the two armies were collected together the Bat **hesitated**[②] which to join. The Birds that passed his **perch**[③] said: "Come with us"; but he said: "I am a Beast." Later on, some Beasts who were passing underneath him looked up and said: "Come with us"; but he said: "I am a Bird." Luckily at the last moment peace was made, and no battle took place, so the Bat came to the Birds and wished to join in the **rejoicings**[④], but they all turned against him and he had to **fly away**[⑤]. He then went to the Beasts, but soon had to beat a **retreat**[⑥], or else they would have torn him to pieces. "Ah," said the Bat, "I see now, he that is neither one thing nor the other has no friends."

---

① conflict /ˈkɔnflikt/ *n.* 冲突,矛盾,争执
② hesitate /ˈheziteit/ *v.* 犹豫,迟疑,踌躇
③ perch /pəːtʃ/ *n.* 栖息处
④ rejoicing /riˈdʒɔisiŋ/ *n.* 欣喜,高兴,欢欣之事
⑤ fly away 飞走
⑥ retreat /riˈtriːt/ *n.* 撤退

二四　熊和两个行人

　　两个人结伴出行，路上忽然碰到一只熊，一个人抢先爬上树,藏到了树枝后面。另一个人眼看自己难以幸免，就倒在地上装死。熊走到他跟前，用鼻子把他从头闻到了脚，他屏住呼吸，尽量装死。没一会儿，熊走了，据说熊从不碰尸体。等熊走远以后，那个人从树上下来，故作幽默地问他的朋友，熊在他耳边说了些什么，他的朋友答道："熊建议我以后千万不要和那种不能共患难的朋友同行。"

　　患难见真交。

XXIV   The Bear and the Two Travelers

Two Men were traveling together, when a Bear suddenly met them on their path. One of them climbed up quickly into a tree and **concealed**① himself in the branches. The other, seeing that he must be attacked, fell flat on the ground, and when the Bear came up and felt him with his **snout**②, and smelt him all over, he held his breath, and **feigned**③ the appearance of death as much us he could. The Bear soon left him, for it is said he will not touch a dead body. When he was quite gone, the other Traveler **descended**④ from the tree, and **jocularly**⑤ **inquired of**⑥ his friend what it was the Bear had **whispered**⑦ in his ear. "He gave me this advice," his companion replied, "Never travel with a friend who deserts you at the approach of danger."

Misfortune⑧ tests the **sincerity**⑨ of friends.

---

① conceal /kən'siːl/ v. 隐藏
② snout /snaut/ n. 鼻口部，鼻子
③ feign /fein/ v. 假装，装作
④ descend /di'send/ v. 降
⑤ jocularly /'dʒɔkjuləli/ a. 好笑地，滑稽地
⑥ inquire of 探问
⑦ whisper /'(h)wispə/ v. 耳语，密谈
⑧ misfortune /mis'fɔːtʃən/ n. 不幸，灾祸
⑨ sincerity /sin'seriti/ n. 诚实，真实，诚心诚意

二五　蜜蜂和朱庇特

　　一只蜂后从伊米托斯山飞到奥林匹斯山，向朱庇特神献上从自己的蜂房采的新鲜蜂蜜。朱庇特见到贡品很开心，就答应蜂后，无论她提出什么愿望，都可以得到满足。于是，蜂后便恳求道："神啊，请你赐给我一根蜇人的刺，如果有人胆敢靠近我的蜂房，取走我的蜂蜜，我便要杀了他。"热爱人类的朱庇特听了这话很不高兴，但他已经有言在先，不能拒绝蜂后的请求，于是就答道："你可以得到你要的刺，但要用你自己的性命来承担后果。如果你用刺伤人，刺就会留在你弄出的伤口里，没有了刺，你也会死掉。"

　　居心叵测的人到头来自食恶果。

XXV   The Bee and Jupiter

A Bee from Mount Hymettus, the queen of the hive, ascended to Olympus to present Jupiter some **honey**① fresh from her honeycomb. Jupiter, delighted with the offering of honey, promised to give whatever she should ask. She therefore besought him, saying, "Give me, I pray thee, a sting, that if any **mortal**② shall approach to take my honey, I may kill him." Jupiter was much **displeased**③, for he loved the **race**④ of man, but could not refuse the request because of his promise. He thus answered the Bee: "You shall have your request, but it will be at the **peril**⑤ of your own life. For if you use your sting, it shall remain in the wound you make, and then you will die from the loss of it."

Evil wishes, like chickens, come home to **roost**⑥.

---

① honey /'hʌni/ *n.* 蜂蜜
② mortal /'mɔːtl/ *n.* 凡人
③ displeased /dis'pliːzd/ *a.* 不快的
④ race /reis/ *n.* 种族
⑤ peril /'peril/ *n.* 危险，冒险
⑥ roost /ruːst/ *n.* 栖息处

二六 捕鸟人、山鹑和公鸡

捕鸟人刚要坐下来吃晚饭，一个朋友忽然不期而至。捕鸟人因为当天一无所获，捕网是空的，就决定杀一只花斑山鹑来款待客人。这山鹑本是他驯养熟了，用来诱捕猎物的。山鹑苦苦恳求捕鸟人饶自己一命："没有了我，你下次张开网，靠什么来捕鸟呢？谁来唱歌伴你入睡？谁来为你把鸟儿引出来？"捕鸟人听了，就放开了山鹑，去抓一只漂亮的刚长出冠子的年轻公鸡。谁知那公鸡用最诚恳的语气说道："如果你杀了我,谁来向你宣告黎明的到来？谁唤醒你去干一天的工作？谁在早上告诉你该去查看捕鸟网了？"捕鸟人答道："你说得不错，你是一只报时的鸟。但我和我的朋友总得吃晚饭啊！"

迫不得已时，顾不上讲理。

XXVI　The　Birdcatcher, the Partridge, and the Cock

　　A Birdcatcher was about to sit down to a dinner of herbs when a friend **unexpectedly**① came in. The bird-trap was quite empty, as he had caught nothing, and he had to kill a pied Partridge, which he had **tamed**② for a **decoy**③. The bird **entreated**④ earnestly for his life: "What would you do without me when next you spread your nets? Who would chirp you to sleep, or call for you the covey of answering birds?" The Birdcatcher spared his life, and determined to **pick out**⑤ a fine young Cock just attaining to his comb. But the Cock **expostulated**⑥ in **piteous**⑦ tones from his perch: "If you kill me, who will announce to you the appearance of the dawn? Who will wake you to your daily tasks or tell you when it is time to visit the bird-trap in the morning?" He replied, "What you say is true. You are a capital bird at telling the time of day. But my friend and I must have our dinners."

　　Necessity knows no law.

---

① unexpectedly /ˈʌniksˈpektidli/ ad. 未料到地,意外地

② tame /teim/ v. 驯养,使……驯服

③ decoy /diˈkɔi/ n. 引诱

④ entreat /inˈtriːt/ v. 恳求,乞求

⑤ pick out 挑出

⑥ expostulate /iksˈpɔstjuleit/ v. (对人或行为的)抗议,告诫

⑦ piteous /ˈpitiəs/ a. 哀怨的, 可怜的

二七　盲人和狼崽

有个盲人，无论把什么动物放到他手上，他只要一摸，就能辨认出是哪种动物。有人把一只狼崽交给他，让他摸摸看是什么动物。盲人摸了摸，迟疑地说道："这是一只小狐狸，还是小狼，我说不清。但有一点是可以肯定的，决不能把它放到羊群里去。"

凶恶的本性即使在幼年也会暴露无遗。

XXVII　The Blind Man and the Whelp①

A Blind Man was **accustomed to**② **distinguishing**③ different animals by touching them with his hands. The whelp of a Wolf was brought to him, with a request that he would feel it, and say what it was. He felt it, and being in doubt, said: "I do not quite know whether it is the cub of a Fox, or the whelp of a Wolf, but this I know full well. It would not be safe to **admit**④ him to the **sheepfold**.⑤ "

Evil **tendencies**⑥ are shown in early life.

---

① whelp /(h)welp/ *n.* 崽，幼兽
② be accustomed to　习惯于
③ admit /əd'mit/ *v.* 允许进入
④ sheepfold /ʃiːpfəuld/ *n.* 羊圈
⑤ tendency /'tendənsi/ *n.* 倾向

二八 吹牛的旅行者

有个人从国外旅行归来，逢人就吹嘘自己在国外立下无数丰功伟绩。他说自己在罗得岛上曾奋力一跳，距离之远，当世无人能及，当时在场的许多目击者都可以来为他作证。这时，有个看热闹的人打断了他的话，说道："老兄，如果你说的都是真的，也就用不着什么证人了，假设这里就是罗得岛，你跳给我们看吧。"

真正成功的人根本不需要自我吹嘘。

XXVIII The Boasting Traveler

A Man who had traveled in foreign lands **boasted**① very much, on returning to his own country, of the many wonderful and heroic feats he had performed in the different places he had visited. Among other things, he said that when he was at Rhodes he had **leaped**② to such a distance that no man of his day could leap anywhere near him as to that, there were in Rhodes many persons who saw him do it and whom he could call as **witnesses**③. One of the **bystanders**④ interrupted him, saying: "Now, my good man, if this be all true there is no need of witnesses. Suppose this to be Rhodes, and leap for us."

He who does a thing well does not need to boast.

---

① boast /bəust/ *v.* 吹牛，自夸
② leap /liːp/ *v.* 跳跃
③ witness /'witnis/ *n.* 目击者，证人
④ bystander /'baistændə/ *n.* 旁观者

二九　男孩和榛子

　　有个男孩伸手到罐子里去拿榛子，抓了满满一大把，当他想把手从罐子里拿出来的时候，却被罐口卡住了。男孩不想丢开手里的榛子，可是手又卡在罐子里出不来，于是哇哇大哭起来，一边哭，一边抱怨自己真倒霉。一个过路人对他说："要是你只拿半把榛子，你的手早就从罐里出来了。"

　　切莫急功近利，贪婪的结果是欲速则不达。

XXIX　The Boy and the Filberts①

　　A Boy put his hand into a **pitcher**② full of filberts. He **grasped**③ as many as he could possibly hold, but when he tried ot pull out his hand, he was prevented from doing so by the **neck**④ of the pitcher. Unwilling to lose his filberts, and yet unable to **withdraw**⑤ his hand, he **burst into tears**⑥ and bitterly lamented his disappointment. A bystander said to him, "Be satisfied with half the **quantity**⑦, and you will **readily**⑧ draw out your hand."

　　Do not **attempt**⑨ too much at once.

---

① filbert /'filbət/ *n.* 榛子
② pitcher /'pitʃə/ *n.* 罐
③ grasp /grɑːsp/ *v.* 抓住
④ neck /nek/ *n.* 脖子，颈
⑤ withdraw /wið'drɔː/ *v.* 撤回，取回
⑥ burst into tears 突然哭起来
⑦ quantity /'kwɔntiti/ *n.* 量，数量
⑧ readily /'redili/ *ad.* 轻易地
⑨ attempt /ə'tempt/ *v.* 企图，试图

三〇 洗澡的男孩

有个男孩在河里洗澡，快要被河水淹死了。他向岸上经过的行人高声呼救，那人非但没有伸出援手，反而安安稳稳地站在那里，责备男孩太不小心。小男孩大喊："先生，求你先把我救上岸去，再骂我也不迟！"

不肯伸出援手，再多的说教也无济于事。

XXX The Boy Bathing

A Boy bathing in a river was in danger of being **drowned**①. He called out to a passing traveler for help, but instead of holding out a helping hand, the man stood by **unconcernedly**②, and **scolded**③ the boy for his **imprudence**④. "Oh, sir！" cried the youth, "pray help me now and scold me afterwards."

Counsel⑤ without help is **useless**⑥.

---

① drown /draun/ *v.* 淹死
② unconcernedly /'ʌnkən'səːndli/ *ad.* 不在乎地，漠不关心地
③ scold /skəuld/ *v.* 责骂，训斥
④ imprudence /im'pruːdəns/ *n.* 轻率，不小心，不谨慎
⑤ counsel /'kaunsəl/ *n.* 忠告
⑥ useless /'juːslis/ *a.* 无用的

三一 捉蝗虫的男孩

有个男孩捉住了许多蝗虫。他看到一只蝎子，误以为是蝗虫，伸手就要去捉。蝎子亮出了毒刺，说道："朋友，如果你敢碰我一下，你不但会失去我，还会失去你所有的蝗虫！"

XXXI The Boy Hunting Locusts

A Boy was hunting for **locusts**①. He had caught a goodly number, when he saw a **Scorpion**②, and mistaking him for a locust, reached out his hand to take him. The Scorpion, showing his **sting**③, said："If you had but touched me, my friend, you would have lost me, and all your locusts too！"

---

① locust /'ləukəst/ *n.* 蝗虫

② scorpion /'skɔːpiən/ *n.* 蝎子

③ sting /stiŋ/ *n.* 刺

三二　男孩和青蛙

几个男孩在池塘边玩耍，看到水里有几只青蛙，就扔石头打青蛙。他们一连砸死了好几只青蛙，这时，一只青蛙从水里冒出头来，对他们喊道："住手吧，孩子们！你们的游戏会要了我们的命！"

你的快乐或许就是别人的痛苦。

XXXII　The Boys and the Frogs

Some Boys, playing near a pond, saw a number of Frogs in the water and began to **pelt**① them with stones. They killed several of them, when one of the Frogs, **lifting**② his head out of the water, cried out: "Pray stop, my boys: what is **sport**③ to you, is death to us."

One man's **pleasure**④ may be another's pain.

---

① pelt /pelt/ *v.* 投掷
② lift /lift/ *v.* 举起
③ sport /spɔːt/ *n.* 游戏
④ pleasure /'pleʒə/ *n.* 高兴，愉快

三三　一捆木棒

有个老人临终时把几个儿子叫到身边，给他们留遗言。他命仆人取来一捆木棒，对长子说："你来把这捆木棒折断。"他的长子用了很大力气，一捆木棒依然完好无损。老人的其他儿子也试着去折，但都失败了。老人说："你们每人从中抽出一根木棒来。"儿子们照着老人的话做了，于是老人又说："现在再折折看。"每根木棒都被轻易折断了。老人说道："这就是我要告诉你们的道理。"

团结力量大。

XXXIII　The Bundle of Sticks

An old man on the point of death **summoned**① his sons around him to give them some parting advice. He ordered his **servants**② to bring in a **faggot**③ of sticks, and said to his eldest son："Break it." The son strained and **strained**④, but with all his efforts was unable to break the bundle. The other sons also tried, but none of them was successful. "**Untie**⑤ the faggots," said the father, "and each of you take a stick." When they had done so, he called out to them："Now, break," and each stick was easily broken. "You see my meaning," said their father.

Union gives strength.

---

① summon /ˈsʌmən/ *v.* 召唤，召集
② servant /ˈsəːvənt/ *n.* 仆人
③ faggot /ˈfægət/ *n.* 柴捆，枝条捆
④ strain /strein/ *v.* 竭尽全力
⑤ untie /ˈʌnˈtai/ *v.* 解开

三四　笼中鸟和蝙蝠

　　挂在窗外的鸟笼里关着一只会唱歌的鸟，但这只鸟只在夜里等其他鸟都熟睡的时候才开口唱歌。有天晚上飞来了一只蝙蝠，他站在鸟笼的栅栏上，问鸟为什么白天沉默不语，只在晚上歌唱？鸟儿答道："这是大有原因的。以前我是在白天唱歌，猎人被我的歌声吸引，用网捉住了我。从那以后，我就只在晚上才唱歌。"蝙蝠说："既然你现在已经成了囚徒，白天不唱也无济于事了。如果你在被人抓住之前就只在晚上才唱歌，可能现在你还是只自由的鸟呢！"

　　未雨绸缪胜过亡羊补牢。

XXXIV The Cage Bird and the Bat

　　A singing bird was **confined**① in a cage which hung outside a window, and had a way of singing at night when all other birds were asleep. One night a Bat came and **clung**② to the bars of the cage, and asked the Bird why she was silent by day and sang only at night. "I have a very good reason for doing so," said the Bird. "It was once when I was singing in the daytime that a **fowler**③ was attracted by my voice, and set his nets for me and caught me. Since then I have never sung except at night." But the Bat replied, "It is no use your doing that now when you are a **prisoner**④: if only you had done so before you were caught, you might still have been free."

　　Precautions⑤ are useless after the **crisis**⑥.

---

① confine /'kɔnfain/ v. 限制,闭居　　② cling /kliŋ/ v. 紧抓
③ fowler /'faulə/ n. 捕野禽者　　④ prisoner /'priznə/ n. 囚犯
⑤ precaution /pri'kɔːʃən/ n. 预防　　⑥ crisis /'kraisis/ n. 危机

三五　骆驼

有个人第一次见到骆驼时，看到骆驼体形硕大，吓得拔腿就跑。过了一段时间，他发现骆驼脾气温和，就鼓起勇气接近骆驼。此后不久，他看到骆驼根本就没有精神，于是就大着胆子给骆驼套上了嚼子，把他交给一个小孩子牵着。

熟悉能够克服恐惧。

XXXV　The Camel

When Man first saw a **Camel**①, he was so **frightened**② at his vast size that he ran away. After a time, **perceiving**③ the **meekness**④ and **gentleness**⑤ of the beast's **temper**⑥, he summoned courage enough to approach him. Soon afterwards, observing that he was an animal altogether **deficient**⑦ in spirit, he assumed such **boldness**⑧ as to put a **bridle**⑨ in his mouth, and to let a child drive him.

Use serves to overcome **dread**⑩.

---

① camel /'kæməl/ *n.* 骆驼
② frighten /'fraitn/ *v.* 使惊吓，惊恐
③ perceive /pə'si:v/ *v.* 察觉
④ meekness /'mi:knis/ *n.* 温顺
⑤ gentleness /'dʒentlnis/ *n.* 温和，温柔
⑥ temper /'tempə/ *n.* 脾气
⑦ deficient /di'fiʃənt/ *a.* 不足的，不充分的
⑧ boldness /'bəuldnis/ *n.* 大胆
⑨ bridle /'braidl/ *n.* 马勒
⑩ dread /dred/ *n.* 恐惧

三六　骆驼和朱庇特

　　骆驼见公牛长着漂亮的牛角，心里非常羡慕，希望自己也能生出同样的角。他来到朱庇特面前，求神赐给自己一对角。朱庇特看到骆驼不满足于自己的身材和力气，还想要求更多的东西，不禁大为恼火，不仅没有给骆驼一对角，还把骆驼的耳朵削去了一截。

　　因为贪婪而羡慕别人，会连本属于自己的东西也失掉。

XXXVI　The Camel and Jupiter

　　The Camel, when he saw the Bull **adorned**① with horns, envied him and wished that he himself could obtain the same horns. He went to Jupiter, and besought him to give him horns. Jupiter, **vexed**② at his request because he was not satisfied with his size and **strength**③ of body, and desired yet more, not only refused to give him **horns**④, but even **deprived**⑤ him of a portion of his ears.

　　By asking for too much, we may lose the little that we once had.

---

① adorn /ə'dɔːn/ *v.* 装饰，佩戴
② vex /veks/ *v.* 恼怒
③ strength /streŋθ/ *n.* 力量
④ horn /hɔːn/ *n.* 角
⑤ deprive /di'praiv/ *v.* 剥夺

三七　猫和鸟

猫听说饲养场里的鸟病了，就乔装改扮成医生，拿着医生用的手杖和提包，跑到饲养场来。他敲敲鸟舍的门，询问鸟的病情，说自己很愿意为生病的鸟治病。里面的鸟回答说："我们现在很好，以后也会过得不错，只要你识相点，快走开。"

XXXVII　The Cat and the Birds

A Cat, hearing that the Birds in a certain **aviary**① were ailing dressed himself up as a **physician**②, and, taking his **cane**③ and a bag of **instruments**④ becoming his profession, went to call on them. He knocked at the door and inquired of the **inmates**⑤ how they all did, saying that if they were ill, he would be happy to **prescribe**⑥ for them and cure them. They replied, "We are all very well, and shall continue so, if you will only be good enough to go away, and leave us as we are."

---

① aviary /'eiviəri/ *n.* 大鸟笼，鸟舍
② physician /fi'ziʃən/ *n.* 内科医生
③ cane /kein/ *n.* 手杖
④ instrument /'instrumənt/ *n.* 仪器
⑤ inmate /'inmeit/ *n.* 同住者
⑥ prescribe /pris'kraib/ *v.* 开药方

三八　猫和公鸡

猫抓住了一只公鸡，想找一个正当的借口吃了他，就指责公鸡在半夜里喔喔叫，打扰人们睡觉。公鸡辩解说，自己啼叫是为了唤醒人们起床去干一天的工作，是为了大家好。猫答道："凭你有再多冠冕堂皇的理由，也不能让我饿肚子。"于是就把公鸡吃了。

XXXVIII The Cat and the Cock

A Cat caught a Cock, and **pondered**① how he might find a reasonable excuse for eating him. He **accused**② him **of** being a **nuisance**③ to men by crowing in the nighttime and not **permitting**④ them to sleep. The Cock **defended**⑤ himself by saying that he did this for the benefit of men, that they might rise in time for their labors. The Cat replied, "Although you **abound**⑥ in **specious**⑦ **apologies**⑧, I shall not remain supperless"; and he made a meal of him.

---

① ponder /'pɔndə/ v. 沉思,考虑
② accuse of 控告
③ nuisance /'njuːsns/ n. 讨厌的东西,讨厌的人
④ permit /pə'mit/ v. 允许,许可
⑤ defend /di'fend/ v. 辩护
⑥ abound /ə'baund/ v. 富于,充满
⑦ specious /'spiːʃəs/ a. 似是而非的,华而不实的
⑧ apology /ə'pɔlədʒi/ n. 辩角,辩护

三九　猫和维纳斯

猫爱上了一位英俊的青年，恳求维纳斯把她变成一个女人。维纳斯答应了猫的要求，把她变成了一个漂亮姑娘。青年看到她，就爱上了她，娶了她做自己的新娘。正当两人躺在新房时，维纳斯想看看变成人的猫是不是连自己的生活习性也改变了，就把一只老鼠放进了屋子。新娘一看到老鼠，立刻就忘了自己现在已经是人了，从卧榻上跳起来向老鼠扑过去，想把它抓来吃掉。维纳斯非常失望，把她又变回了原来的形状。

这是说本性难移。

XXXIX   The Cat and Venus

A Cat fell in love with a handsome young man, and entreated Venus to change her into the **form**① of a woman. Venus **consented**② to her request and transformed her into a beautiful **damsel**③, so that the youth saw her and loved her, and took her home as his **bride**④. While the two were **reclining**⑤ in their chamber, Venus wishing to discover if the Cat in her change of shape had also altered her habits of life, let down a mouse in the middle of the room. The Cat, quite forgetting her present condition, started up from the couch and **pursued**⑥ the mouse, wishing to eat it. Venus was much disappointed and again caused her to return to her former shape.

Nature **exceeds**⑦ nurture.

---

① form /fɔːm/ *n.* 形状　　　　　② consent /kən'sent/ *v.* 同意
③ damsel /'dæmzəl/ *n.* 年轻女人　④ bride /braid/ *n.* 新娘
⑤ recline /ri'klain/ *v.* 靠在，斜倚，倚靠　⑥ pursue /pə'sjuː/ *v.* 追捕
⑦ exceed /ik'siːd/ *v.* 超过，胜过

四〇 烧炭人和漂洗工

有个烧炭人在自己家里烧炭。有一天，他遇到一个当漂洗工的朋友，就请他搬来与自己同住，并说两人不但可以成为好邻居，还可以省下一笔房租。漂洗工答道："我觉得这主意不可行，凡是我漂白了的东西，你的煤烟立刻就会把它熏黑。"

物以类聚，人以群分。

XL The Charcoal-Burner and the Fuller

A Charcoal-Burner carried on his trade in his own house. One day he met a friend, a Fuller, and **entreated**① him to come and live with him, saying that they should be far better neighbors and that their **housekeeping**② expenses would be **lessened**③. The Fuller replied, "The **arrangement**④ is impossible as far as I am **concerned**⑤, for whatever I should **whiten**⑥, you would immediately blacken again with your **charcoal**⑦."

Like will **draw**⑧ like.

---

① entreat /in'tri:t/ v. 恳求,乞求
② housekeeping /'haʊski:piŋ/ n. 家事,家政
③ lessen /'lesn/ v. 减少,变小
④ arrangement /ə'reindʒmənt/ n. 安排
⑤ concern /kən'sɜːn/ v. 涉及,与……有关
⑥ whiten /'(h)waitn/ v. 使……白
⑦ charcoal /'tʃaːkəʊl/ n. 木炭,炭笔
⑧ draw /drɔː/ v. (drew,drawn) 吸引

四一 战马和磨坊主

一匹年老体衰的战马不能再上战场了，就被送到磨坊里干活。被迫拉磨的战马想着从前的日子，不禁哀叹命运无常："磨坊主啊，我以前驰骋沙场，从前胸到尾巴伤痕累累，但是有人精心照料。我现在看不出磨坊有哪一点比战场好。"磨坊主答道："别老拿陈年旧事唠叨个没完，命运起起伏伏是世间常情。"

XLI The Charger and the Miller

A Charger, feeling the **infirmities**① of age, was sent to work in a mill instead of going out to battle. But when he was **compelled**② to **grind**③ instead of serving in the wars, he **bewailed**④ his change of fortune and called to mind his former state, saying, "Ah! Miller, I had indeed to go **campaigning**⑤ before, but I was **barbed**⑥ from counter to tail, and a man went along to **groom**⑦ me, and now I cannot understand what ailed me to prefer the mill before the battle." "**Forbear**⑧," said the Miller to him, "**harping**⑨ on what was of **yore**⑩, for it is the common lot of mortals to **sustain**⑪ the ups and downs of fortune."

---

① infirmity /in'fə:miti/ *n.* 虚弱，衰弱
② compel /kəm'pel/ *v.* 强迫，迫使
③ grind /graind/ *v.* 碾碎，磨碎
④ bewail /bi'weil/ *v.* 悲叹，伤感
⑤ campaign /kæm'pein/ *v.* 参加战役
⑥ barb /bɑ:b/ *v.* 钩
⑦ groom /grum/ *v.* 喂马
⑧ forbear /'fɔ:'bɛə/ *v.* 忍耐，克制
⑨ harp /hɑ:p/ *v.* 反复诉说，唠叨
⑩ yore /jɔ:/ *n.* 昔日
⑪ sustain /səs'tein/ *v.* 承受，经受

四二　公鸡和珍珠

　　场院里的公鸡在一群母鸡旁边趾高气扬地走来走去，忽然发现草丛里有个东西在闪闪发光，公鸡大叫一声："喔喔喔，那是我的!"他拨开草丛，发现那是一颗珍珠，是有人不小心丢在院子里的。公鸡说："喜欢珍珠的人可能会认为这是个宝贝，但我宁可用满满一袋子珍珠来换一粒大麦。"

　　珍贵的东西要有人欣赏才有价值。

XLII The Cock and the Pearl①

A Cock was once **strutting**② up and down the **farmyard**③ among the hens when suddenly he **espied**④ something shinning **amid**⑤ the **straw**⑥. "Ho! Ho!" quoth he, "that's for me," and soon rooted it out from beneath the straw. What did it turn out to be but a Pearl that by some chance had been lost in the yard. "You may be a treasure," quoth Master Cock, "to men that prize you, but for me I would rather have a single barley-corn than a **peck**⑦ of pearls."

Precious things are for those that can prize them.

---

① pearl /pə:l/ *n.* 珍珠
② strut /strʌt/ *v.* 趾高气扬地走
③ farmyard /'fɑ:mjɑ:d/ *n.* 农家场院
④ espy /is'pai/ *v.* (从远处等)突然看到
⑤ amid /ə'mid/ *prep.* 在其间,在其中
⑥ straw /strɔ:/ *n.* 稻草
⑦ peck /pek/ *n.* 配克(2加仑或9升)

四三　螃蟹母子

一只螃蟹对儿子说："你为什么总是横着走，我的孩子？应该直着走才对呀！"小螃蟹答道："你说得对，好妈妈。如果你能直着走一次让我看看，我今后一定直着走。"螃蟹妈妈试了试，没有成功，从此不再纠正儿子走路的方法了。

榜样的力量胜过说教。

XLIII　The Crab and Its Mother

A **Crab**① said to her son, "Why do you walk so one-sided, my child? It is far more becoming to **go straight forward**②." The young Crab replied: "Quite true, dear Mother; and if you will show me the straight way, I will promise to walk in it." The Mother tried in vain, and submitted without **remonstrance**④ to the **reproof**⑤ of her child.

Example is more powerful than **precept**⑥.

---

① crab /kræb/ *n.* 蟹
② go straight forward 直着走
③ in vain 徒然(白费,无效)
④ remonstrance /ri'mɔnstrəns/ *n.* 抗议,抱怨
⑤ reproof /ri'pru:f/ *n.* 斥责,责备
⑥ precept /'pri:sept/ *n.* 教训,告诫,训诫

四四 螃蟹和狐狸

螃蟹离开了海边，在附近一片绿草地上安了家。饥饿的狐狸跑过来，一口咬住了螃蟹。眼见自己性命不保，螃蟹叹道："我真是自作自受。我天生只适合住在海里，干吗要跑到陆地上来呢？"

满足现状的人才会快乐。

XLIV   The Crab and the Fox

A Crab, **forsaking** ① the seashore, chose a neighboring green meadow as its feeding ground. A Fox came across him, and being very hungry ate him up. Just as he was on the point of being eaten, the Crab said, "I well deserve my **fate**②, for what business had I on the land, when by my nature and habits I am only **adapted**③ for the sea?"

Contentment④ with our lot is an **element**⑤ of happiness.

---

① forsake /fə'seik/ v. 放弃,抛弃
② fate /feit/ n. 命运
③ adapt /ə'dæpt/ v. 使……适应
④ contentment /kən'tentmənt/ n. 满足
⑤ element /'elimənt/ n. 成分,要素,元素

四五　乌鸦和墨丘利

　　一只落网的乌鸦求阿波罗神帮他脱困，许诺向神庙献上乳香。可是当他脱离危险后就忘记了自己的誓言。不久以后，乌鸦又陷入了罗网，这次他不再求阿波罗，转而向墨丘利神求救，也许诺向神庙献上乳香。乌鸦的话音刚落，墨丘利就出现在他面前，对他说道："你这个最可恶的家伙！你欺骗了搭救你的恩人，又背叛了他，教我怎么能相信你呢？"

XLV　The Crow and Mercury

　　A Crow caught in a **snare**① prayed to Apollo to **release**② him, making a **vow**③ to offer some **frankincense**④ at his shrine. But when rescued from his danger, he forgot his promise. Shortly afterwards, again caught in a snare, he passed by Apollo and made the same promise to offer frankincense to Mercury. Mercury soon **appeared**⑤ and said to him, "O thou most base fellow! How can I believe thee, who **hast**⑥ disowned and wronged thy former **patron**⑦?"

---

① snare /snɛə/ *n.* 陷阱
② release /ri'liːs/ *v.* 释放
③ vow /vau/ *n.* 誓约
④ frankincense /'fræŋkinsens/ *n.* 乳香
⑤ appear /ə'piə/ *v.* 出现
⑥ hast /hæst/ *v.* have的第二人称单数现在式
⑦ patron /'peitrən/ *n.* 赞助人

四六　乌鸦和蛇

一只焦急寻找食物的乌鸦看到一条蛇正躺在太阳地里睡觉，就猛扑下来一把抓住了蛇。蛇回过头来，狠狠咬了乌鸦一口。垂死的乌鸦叹道："我真是不幸！原以为发现了意外的美食，谁知竟为此送了性命。"

XLVI　The Crow and the Serpent

A Crow in great want of food saw a Serpent asleep in a sunny **nook**[1], and flying down, **greedily**[2] seized him. The Serpent, turning about, bit the Crow with a mortal wound. In the **agony**[3] of death, the bird **exclaimed**[4]: "O unhappy me! Who have found in that which I deemed a happy windfall the source of my **destruction**[5]."

[1] nook /nuk/ *n.* 角落，躲蔽处，隐匿处
[2] greedily /'griːdili/ *ad.* 贪食地，贪婪地
[3] agony /'ægəni/ *n.* (极度的)痛苦，创痛
[4] exclaim /iks'kleim/ *v.* 大叫，呼喊
[5] destruction /dis'trʌkʃən/ *n.* 毁灭

四七　母鹿和狮子

母鹿被猎人紧紧追赶，慌忙中躲进了狮子洞。狮子看见母鹿跑来，就藏了起来，等到母鹿以为自己在洞里安全了，才扑上去把她撕成了碎片。母鹿哀叹道："我真不幸! 才躲开了猎人，又把自己送到了野兽的嘴里。"

避难的人一定得当心不要陷入另一重劫难。

XLVII　The Doe and the Lion

A Doe hard pressed by hunters sought **refuge**① in a cave belonging to a Lion. The Lion concealed himself on seeing her **approach**②, but when she was safe **within**③ the cave, sprang upon her and tore her to pieces. "Woe is me," **exclaimed**④ the Doe, "who have **escaped**⑤ from man, only to throw myself into the mouth of a wild beast! "

In **avoiding**⑥ one evil, care must be taken not to fall into another.

---

① refuge /'refjuːdʒ/ *n.* 避难(处)，庇护(所)
② approach /ə'prəʊtʃ/ *v.* 靠近，接近
③ within /wið'in/ *prep.* 在……里面
④ exclaim /iks'kleim/ *v.* 大叫，呼喊
⑤ escape from 逃离
⑥ avoid /ə'vɔid/ *v.* 避免

四八　狗和野兔

猎狗在山坡上发现了一只野兔，就在后面穷追不舍。他一会儿用牙齿咬住野兔，好像要吃了她；一会儿又对野兔摇摇尾巴，好像自己是在同另一只狗玩耍。野兔对猎狗说："我希望你对我认真一点，让我看看你的真面目。如果你是我的朋友，为什么要狠狠地咬我；如果你是我的敌人，又为什么要对我摇尾巴？"

如果你不知道该不该信任一个人，就别和他做朋友。

XLVIII　The Dog and the Hare

A **Hound**① having started a **Hare**② on the **hillside**③ pursued her for some distance, at one time biting her with his teeth as if he would take her life, and at another **fawning**④ upon her, as if in play with another dog. The Hare said to him, "I wish you would act **sincerely**⑤ by me, and show yourself in your true colors. If you are a friend, why do you bite me so hard? If an enemy, why do you fawn on me?"

No one can be a friend if you know not **whether**⑥ to trust or distrust him.

---

① hound /haund/ *n.* 猎犬
② hare /hɛə/ *n.* 野兔
③ hillside /'hilsaid/ *n.* (小山)山腰, 山坡
④ fawn /fɔːn/ *v.* 巴结, 奉承
⑤ sincerely /sin'siəli/ *ad.* 真诚地
⑥ whether /'(h)weðə/ *conj.* 是否

四九　狗和牡蛎

一只爱吃鸡蛋的狗看见了一只牡蛎，以为是鸡蛋，就张开大嘴把牡蛎一口吞了下去，而且吃得津津有味。过了没多久，狗觉得胃里一阵剧痛，就对自己说道："我活该受苦，谁让我傻到以为圆的东西都是鸡蛋呢!"

做事不经大脑的人往往会陷入意想不到的危险。

XLIX　The Dog and the Oyster

A Dog, used to eating eggs, saw an **Oyster**① and, opening his mouth to its widest extent, **swallowed**② it down with the **utmost**③ **relish**④, supposing it to be an egg. Soon afterwards suffering great pain in his **stomach**⑤, he said, "I deserve all this **torment**⑥, for my **folly**⑦ in thinking that everything round must be an egg."

They who act without **sufficient**⑧ thought, will often fall into unsuspected danger.

---

① oyster /'ɔistə/ *n.* 牡蛎
② swallow /'swɔləu/ *v.* 吞下，咽下
③ utmost /'ʌtməust/ *a.* 极度的
④ relish /'reliʃ/ *n.* 滋味
⑤ stomach /'stʌmək/ *n.* 胃
⑥ torment /'tɔːment/ *n.* 苦痛
⑦ folly /'fɔli/ *n.* 愚蠢，荒唐事
⑧ sufficient /sə'fiʃənt/ *a.* 足够的，充分的

五〇　食槽里的狗

　　一只狗找地方睡午觉，就跳进了牛的食槽，趴在干草堆上舒舒服服地睡着了。不久，牛干完了下午的活，走到食槽边来吃草，惊醒了狗的好梦。愤怒的狗跳起来对着牛汪汪狂吠，只要牛一靠近食槽，狗就威胁着要咬他。最后，牛只好放弃了吃草的念头，转身走开了，一边走一边小声嘟囔："哎，有人霸占着好东西，自己不能享用，也不许别人用。"

L　The Dog in the Manger

A Dog looking out for its afternoon nap **jumped**① into the Manger of an Ox and lay there **cosily**② upon the straw. But soon the Ox, returning from its afternoon work, came up to the Manger and wanted to eat some of the straw. The Dog in a rage, being **awakened**③ from its **slumber**④, stood up and **barked**⑤ at the Ox, and whenever it came near attempted to bite it. At last the Ox had to give up the hope of getting at the straw, and went away **muttering**⑥ : "Ah, people often **grudge**⑦ others what they cannot enjoy themselves."

---

① jump /dʒʌmp/ v. 跳越
② cosily /'kəuzili/ ad. 舒适地
③ awaken /ə'weikən/ v. 醒来
④ slumber /'slʌmbə/ n. 睡眠
⑤ bark /bɑːk/ v. 吠，叫
⑥ mutter /'mʌtə/ v. 喃喃自语，作低沉声，出怨言
⑦ grudge /grʌdʒ/ v. 怀恨，嫉妒

五一　狗和倒影

　　一只狗找到了一块肉，把肉叼在嘴里，准备带回家去慢慢享用。在路上，狗要经过一座架在小河上的独木桥，路过那座桥时，他向桥下一望，看见了自己在水里的倒影。狗以为那是另一只狗，嘴里也叼着肉，就想去把那只狗的肉抢过来，于是他冲着水里的狗咬了过去，谁知他刚一张嘴，嘴里的那块肉应声掉进了水里，被水冲走了。

　　这是说不要为了追逐幻影，最终把原本拥有的也丢了。

LI　The Dog and the Shadow

　　It happened that a Dog had got a piece of meat and was carrying it home in his mouth to eat it **in peace**①. Now on his way home he had to cross a plank lying across a running **brook**②. As he crossed, he looked down and saw his own shadow reflected in the water beneath. Thinking it was another dog with another piece of meat, he made up his mind to have that also. So he made a **snap**③ at the shadow in the water, but as he opened his mouth the piece of meat fell out, dropped into the water and was never seen more.

　　Beware④ lest you lose the substance by grasping at the shadow.

---

① in peace 安详地
② brook /bruk/ *n.* 小河，溪
③ snap /snæp/ *n.* 突然咬住
④ beware /bi'wɛə/ *v.* 小心，谨防

五二　狗和牛皮

一群饿狗看见有几张牛皮泡在河里，但是可望而不可即，他们便决定把河水喝干。但直到狗被河水撑破了肚皮，牛皮还漂在离他们很远的水里。

切不可自不量力。

LII The Dog and the Hides

Some Dogs **famished**① with hunger saw a number of **cowhides** ② **steeping**③ in a river. Not being able to reach them, they agreed to drink up the river, but it happened that they burst themselves with drinking long before they reached the hides.

Attempt no impossibilities.

---

① famish /'fæmiʃ/ v. 使挨饿,饥饿,挨饿
② cowhide /'kauhaid/ n. 牛皮
③ steep /stiːp/ v. 浸泡,浸透

五三　海豚、鲸鱼和鲱鱼

海豚和鲸鱼之间爆发了激烈的战争，正当双方打得不可开交之时，一条鲱鱼从水里探出头来，提出如果鲸鱼和海豚同意的话，自己可以作为裁判来替他们调解分歧。一只海豚回答说："我们宁可在战斗中同归于尽，也不愿让你来干涉我们的事情。"

LIII　The Dolphins, the Whales, and the Sprat

The **Dolphins**① and **Whales**② **waged**③ a **fierce**④ war with each other. When the battle was at its **height**⑤, a **Sprat**⑥ lifted its head out of the waves and said that he would reconcile their differences if they would accept him as an **umpire**⑦. One of the Dolphins replied, "We would far rather be destroyed in our battle with each other than admit any **interference**⑧ from you in our affairs."

---

① dolphin /ˈdɔlfin/ *n.* 海豚
② whale /weil/ *n.* 鲸
③ wage /weidʒ/ *v.* 开始，进行（战争、运动）
④ fierce /fiəs/ *a.* 猛烈的
⑤ height /hait/ *n.* 顶点
⑥ sprat /spræt/ *n.* 鲱属的小海鱼
⑦ umpire /ˈʌmpaiə/ *n.* 裁判员
⑧ interference /ˌintəˈfiərəns/ *n.* 干涉

五四　鹰和捕鹰人

有人捉到一只鹰，立刻剪掉了鹰的翅膀，把他放在养鸡场里，同其他的家禽关在一起。鹰受到这样的对待，非常难过。后来，邻居买下这只鹰，鹰的羽翼也逐渐恢复了。鹰展翅高飞，抓到一只野兔，便立刻拿来送给自己的恩人。狐狸看见了，连忙说道："先别忙着向这人邀功请赏，你应该首先去讨好你以前的主人，否则的话，他会再把你抓住，剪掉你的翅膀。"

LIV　The Eagle and His Captor

An **Eagle**① was once captured by a man, who immediately **clipped**② his wings and put him into his poultry-yard with the other birds, at which treatment the Eagle was **weighed**③ down with grief. Later, another neighbor purchased him and allowed his **feathers**④ to grow again. The Eagle took **flight**⑤, and pouncing upon a hare, brought it at once as an offering to his **benefactor**⑥. A Fox, seeing this, exclaimed, "Do not **cultivate**⑦ the favor of this man, but of your former owner, lest he should again hunt for you and **deprive**⑧ you a second time of your wings."

① eagle /'iːgl/ n. 鹰
② clip /klip/ v. 修剪
③ weigh /wei/ v. 重压
④ feather /'feðə/ n. 羽毛
⑤ flight /flait/ n. 飞行
⑥ benefactor /'beniˌfæktə/ n. 恩人
⑦ cultivate /'kʌltiveit/ v. 努力获得(支持或友谊)
⑧ deprive /di'praiv/ v. 剥夺

五五 鹰和箭

一只鹰正展翅高飞，猛然听到弓箭的飕飕声，接着便受了致命伤。鹰慢慢地落到地上，鲜血从伤口喷涌而出。鹰看着射杀自己的羽箭，发现箭杆上有一根自己的羽毛。鹰在临死前仰天长叹："唉，我们常常把毁灭自己的武器交到敌人手上。"

LV The Eagle and the Arrow

An Eagle was **soaring**① through the air when suddenly it heard the **whizz**② of an **Arrow**③, and felt itself wounded to death. Slowly it **fluttered down**④ to the earth, with its life-blood pouring out of it. Looking down upon the Arrow with which it had been **pierced**⑤, it found that the shaft of the Arrow had been feathered with one of its own **plumes**⑥. "Alas! " it cried, as it died, "We often give our enemies the means for our own destruction."

---

① soar /sɔː/ *v.* 往上飞舞
② whizz /hwiz/ *v.* （飕飕地）飞驰
③ arrow /'ærəu/ *n.* 箭
④ flutter down 鼓翅而下
⑤ pierce /piəs/ *v.* 刺穿，穿透
⑥ plume /pluːm/ *n.* 羽毛

五六　农夫和他的儿子

农夫临死时希望儿子们能像自己一样精心照料农场。他把几个儿子都叫到床边，对他们说："孩子们，我在一个葡萄园里藏着许多财宝。"他的儿子们在农夫死后用铁锹和锄头小心翼翼地翻遍了葡萄园里的每一寸土地，虽然没有找到任何财宝，但他们的劳动也得到了回报——这一年的葡萄长得又多又好。

这是说勤劳就是无价之宝。

LVI　The Farmer and His Sons

A Father, being on the point of death, wished to be sure that his sons would give the same attention to his farm as he himself had given it. He called them to his **bedside**① and said, "My sons, there is a great treasure hid in one of my **vineyards**②." The sons, after his death, took their **spades**③ and **mattocks**④ and carefully dug over every portion of their land. They found no treasure, but the vines repaid their labor by an **extraordinary**⑤ and **superabundant**⑥ **crop**⑦.

In the end, industry is truly a treasure itself.

---

① bedside /'bedsaid/ *n.* 床边

② vineyard /'vinjɑːd/ *n.* 葡萄园

③ spade /speid/ *n.* 铲

④ mattock /'mætək/ *n.* 鹤嘴锄之一种

⑤ extraordinary /iks'trɔːdnri/ *a.* 非常的，特别的

⑥ superabundant /sjuːpərə'bʌndənt/ *a.* 过多的，有余的

⑦ crop /krɔp/ *n.* 农作物

五七　农夫和蛇

在冬天里，农夫看到一条被冻僵了的蛇，心地善良的农夫把蛇捡起来，放进自己怀里。温暖让蛇很快就苏醒过来，它露出凶恶的本性，狠狠咬了恩人一口。农夫受了致命伤，临死前哀叹道："这就是我同情恶棍应得的下场。"

即使对恶人仁至义尽，他们也是本性难移。

LVII　The Farmer and the Snake

One Winter a Farmer found a Snake stiff and **frozen**① with cold. He had **compassion**② on it, and taking it up, placed it in his **bosom**③. The Snake was quickly **revived**④ by the warmth, and **resuming**⑤ its natural **instincts**⑥, bit its benefactor, **inflicting**⑦ on him a mortal wound. "Oh," cried the Farmer with his last breath, "I am rightly served for pitying a **scoundrel**⑧."

The greatest kindness will not **bind**⑨ the ungrateful.

---

① frozen /'frəuzn/ *a.* 冰冻的
② compassion /kəm'pæʃən/ *n.* 同情，怜悯
③ bosom /'buzəm/ *n.* 胸部
④ revive /ri'vaiv/ *v.* 使……生醒
⑤ resume /ri'zjuːm/ *v.* 重新得到或占有
⑥ instinct /'instiŋkt/ *n.* 天性
⑦ inflict /in'flikt/ *v.* 加害
⑧ scoundrel /'skaundrəl/ *n.* 无赖
⑨ bind /baind/ *v.* 约束

五八　打架的公鸡和鹰

两只好斗的公鸡为争夺场院打得不可开交。一番激烈的打斗之后，其中一只公鸡落荒而逃。战败者缩在角落里闷闷不乐，胜利者跃上高墙，拍拍翅膀，扯开喉咙兴奋地大声啼叫。天上的老鹰看见了，冲下来一把抓住这只公鸡，带回巢去了。战败的公鸡立刻从角落里跑出来，在场院里当起了无可争辩的主人。

骄者必败。

LVIII　The Fighting Cocks and the Eagle

Two Game Cocks were fiercely fighting for the mastery of the farmyard. One at last put the other to flight. The **vanquished**[1] Cock **skulked**[2] away and hid himself in a quiet corner, while the **conqueror**[3], flying up to a high wall, **flapped**[4] his wings and crowed **exultingly**[5] with all his might. An Eagle sailing through the air pounced upon him and carried him off in his **talons**[6]. The vanquished Cock immediately came out of his corner, and ruled **henceforth**[7] with **undisputed**[8] mastery.

Pride goes before destruction.

---

① vanquish /'væŋkwiʃ/ v. 打败，征服
② skulk /skʌlk/ v. 躲躲闪闪
③ conqueror /'kɔŋkərə/ n. 征服者，胜利者
④ flap /flæp/ v. 拍打，鼓翼而飞
⑤ exultingly /ig'zʌltiŋli/ ad. 兴高采烈地，得意地
⑥ talon /'tælən/ n. 猛禽的爪
⑦ henceforth /hens'fɔ:θ/ ad. 今后
⑧ undisputed /'ʌndis'pju:tid/ a. 无可置辩的，无异议的

五九　渔夫和小鱼

渔夫辛苦了一整天，只捕到一条小鱼。"请放我走吧，老爷，"鱼说道："我太小了，你现在还不能吃我。如果你把我放回河里，我很快就会长大，到时候你可以把我捉来美美地吃上一顿。"渔夫说："不行，不行，我的小鱼，我现在已经抓住你了，以后我可能就捉不到你了。"

抓在手里的东西再小，也胜过美妙的幻想。

LIX   The Fisher and the Little Fish

It happened that a Fisher, after fishing all day, caught only a little fish. "**Pray**①, let me go, master," said the Fish. "I am much too small for your eating just now. If you put me back into the river I shall soon grow, then you can make a fine meal off me."

"Nay, nay, my little Fish," said the Fisher, "I have you now. I may not catch you **hereafter**②."

A little thing in hand is worth more than a great thing in **prospect**③.

---

① pray /prei/ *v.* 恳求，乞求
② hereafter /hiər'ɑːftə/ *n.* 将来
③ prospect /'prɔspekt/ *n.* 展望，想像

六〇 苍蝇和蜂蜜罐

管家的屋子里打碎了一罐蜂蜜，一群苍蝇循着香味飞来，站在蜂蜜里贪婪地大吃。没过多久，苍蝇的脚被蜂蜜粘住了，任凭它们怎么扇动翅膀，也飞不起来，渐渐地，一只只苍蝇都陷入蜂蜜里，被蜜淹死了。垂死的苍蝇哀叹道："我们真愚蠢，为一点小小的享乐送了性命。"

快乐背后往往暗藏着痛苦和伤害。

LX The Flies and the Honey-Pot

A Number of Flies were attracted to a **jar**① of honey which had been **overturned**② in a housekeeper's room, and placing their feet in it, ate greedily. Their feet, however, became so **smeared**③ with the honey that they could not use their wings, nor release themselves, and were **suffocated**④. Just as they were **expiring**⑤, they exclaimed, "O foolish **creatures** ⑥ that we are, for the sake of a little pleasure we have destroyed ourselves."

Pleasure bought with pains, hurts.

---

① jar /dʒɑː/ *n.* 广口瓶

② overturn /ˌəuvəˈtəːn/ *v.* 翻倒，倾覆

③ smear /smiə/ *v.* 涂，擦上

④ suffocate /ˈsʌfəkeit/ *v.* (使)窒息而死

⑤ expire /iksˈpaiə/ *v.* 断气

⑥ creature /ˈkriːtʃə/ *n.* 生物

六一　苍蝇和拉车的骡子

一只苍蝇落在大车的车轴上，对拉车的骡子说："你走得太慢了！为什么不跑快一点？如果你不快跑，我可要叮你的脖子！"骡子回答说："用不着你来吓唬我，我只听从坐在你上头的那个人的命令，他挥鞭子，我就快跑，他拉缰绳，我就止步。所以，收起你那副傲慢的嘴脸吧，我心里很清楚什么时候该快，什么时候该慢。"

LXI　The Fly and the Draught-Mule

A **Fly**① sat on the axle-tree of a **chariot**②, and addressing the Draught-Mule said, "How slow you are! Why do you not go faster? See if I do not prick your neck with my sting." The Draught-Mule replied, "I do not heed your **threats**③; I only care for him who sits above you, and who quickens my pace with his **whip**④, or holds me back with the **reins**⑤. Away, therefore, with your **insolence**⑥, for I know well when to go fast, and when to go slow."

---

① fly /flai/ *n.* 苍蝇
② chariot /ˈtʃæriət/ *n.* 二轮车
③ threat /θret/ *n.* 威胁，恐吓
④ whip /(h)wip/ *n.* 鞭
⑤ rein /rein/ *n.* 缰绳
⑥ insolence /ˈinsələns/ *n.* 傲慢，无礼

六二　捕鸟人和毒蛇

捕鸟人带着粘鸟胶和捕鸟杆出门去抓鸟，他看见一只歌鸫栖在树上，就把手里的捕鸟杆拉长，全神贯注地盯住那只鸟，准备随时出手。就在他一心只顾抬头向上看的时候，不小心踩到了一条正在他脚边熟睡的毒蛇。被惊醒的蛇张口就咬，捕鸟人一下子摔倒在地，自言自语道："真倒霉! 我本来想当猎人，没想到自己却跌进了死亡的陷阱。"

LXII　The Fowler and the Viper

A Fowler, taking his bird-lime and his twigs, went out to catch birds. Seeing a **thrush**① sitting upon a tree, he wished to take it, and fitting his twigs to a proper length, watched **intently**②, having his whole thoughts directed towards the sky. While thus looking **upwards**③, he unknowingly **trod**④ upon a **Viper**⑤ asleep just before his feet. The Viper, turning about, stung him, and falling into a swoon, the man said to himself, "Woe is me! That while I purposed to hunt another, I am myself fallen unawares into the snares of death."

---

① thrush /θrʌʃ/ n. 画眉鸟
② intently /in'tentli/ ad. 一心一意地, 心无旁骛地
③ upwards /'ʌpwədz/ a. 向上的, 上升的
④ trod /trɔd/ v. tread的过去式(分词), 踩
⑤ viper /'vaipə/ n. 毒蛇

六三　狐狸和猫

　　狐狸向猫吹嘘自己足智多谋，可以用很多种方法避开敌人："我有一百种办法可以从敌人面前逃跑。"

　　"我只会一种办法，"猫说道，"但通常很管用。"正说着，他们听到远处传来一群猎狗的叫声，猫三下两下就爬上树，躲进了茂密的枝叶里，对狐狸说："这就是我逃跑的办法，你怎么办呢？"

　　狐狸的办法很多，他想了一种又一种，就在他举棋不定的时候，猎狗已经越来越近了。最后，始终拿不定主意的狐狸被猎狗团团围住，没过多久，猎人赶到，杀死了狐狸。猫看到这一幕，说道："一种安全的办法胜过一百种靠不住的法子。"

LXIII   The Fox and the Cat

A Fox was boasting to a Cat of its clever **devices**① for escaping its enemies. "I have a whole bag of **tricks**②," he said, "which **contains**③ a hundred ways of escaping my enemies."

"I have only one," said the Cat; "but I can generally manage with that." Just at that moment they heard the cry of a pack of hounds coming towards them, and the Cat immediately **scampered**④ up a tree and hid herself in the boughs. "This is my play," said the Cat. "What are you going to do?"

The Fox thought first of one way, then of another, and while he was debating the hounds came nearer and nearer, and at last the Fox in his confusion was caught up by the hounds and soon killed by the huntsmen. Miss Puss, who had been looking on, said: "Better one safe say than a hundred on which you cannot **reckon**⑤."

---

① device /di'vais/ *n.* 策略
② trick /trik/ *n.* 诡计
③ contain /kən'tein/ *v.* 包含
④ scamper /'skæmpə/ *v.* 奔跑,快跑
⑤ reckon /'rekən/ *v.* 指望,依赖

六四　狐狸和刺藤

　　狐狸翻越篱笆的时候失足摔了下来，幸好抓住一株刺藤，才保全了性命。但狐狸的脚底被扎得鲜血淋淋，他埋怨刺藤说，自己本来是向她求救的，不想却被她害得更惨。刺藤打断了狐狸的话，对他说道："凡是我碰到的东西，我都会抓住不放，可现在是你抓着我不肯放手，反来怪我，真是岂有此理！"

　　在自私者眼中，人人都自私。

LXIV　The Fox and the Bramble

　　A Fox was mounting a hedge when he lost his footing and caught hold of a Bramble to save himself. Having pricked and **grievously**① torn the **soles**② of his feet, he accused the Bramble because, when he had fled to her for **assistance**③, she had used him worse than the **hedge**④ itself. The **Bramble**⑤, interrupting him, said, "But you really must have been out of your senses to fasten yourself on me, who am myself always accustomed to **fasten upon**⑥ others."

　　To the selfish all are selfish.

---

① grievously /'gri:vəsli/ *ad.* 痛苦地，严重地

② sole /səul/ *n.* 脚掌

③ assistance /ə'sistəns/ *n.* 帮助，援助

④ hedge /hedʒ/ *n.* 树篱

⑤ bramble /'bræmbəl/ *n.* 荆棘

⑥ fasten upon 握住，抓牢

六五　狐狸和山羊

　　狐狸失足落入一口深井，想尽了办法也逃不出来。过了一会儿，有只山羊路过这里，问狐狸在井底干什么。"难道你还没有听说吗？"狐狸说道，"大旱灾就要来了，我跳到井里是为了让自己有水喝。你为什么不下来呢？"山羊信以为真，也跳到井里。狐狸立刻跳到山羊背上，踩着长长的羊角，跃出了井口，回过头来对山羊说："再见了，朋友，下次一定要记住，陷入困境的人的建议是万万信不得的。"

LXV　The Fox and the Goat

　　By an unlucky chance a Fox fell into a deep well from which he could not **get out**①. A Goat passed by shortly afterwards, and asked the Fox what he was doing down there. "Oh, have you not heard?" said the Fox; "there is going to be a great **drought**②, so I jumped down here in order to be sure to have water by me. Why don't you come down too?" The Goat thought well of this advice, and jumped down into the well. But the Fox immediately jumped on her back, and by putting his foot on her long horns managed to jump up to the edge of the well. "Good-bye, friend," said the Fox, "remember next time, never trust the advice of a man in difficulties."

---

① get out 出去
② drought /draut/ n. 干旱

六六　狐狸和乌鸦

　　乌鸦嘴里叼着一块奶酪，飞到树枝上。狐狸见了，心想："我是一只狐狸，那奶酪应该是我的。"他走到树下，仰起头对乌鸦说："你好啊，乌鸦小姐。你今天的气色真好，你的羽毛多么光彩照人，眼睛多么明亮！我敢肯定，你的歌声和外表一样美，其他的鸟都比不上你。请为我唱一首歌吧，我愿奉你为鸟中之王。"

　　乌鸦听了，昂起头呱呱大叫，可她刚一张口，嘴里的奶酪就掉了下来，狐狸赶紧冲上来，一口咬住奶酪，对乌鸦说："这就对了，我要的就是这个。谢谢你的奶酪，作为回报，我送你一句忠告——千万别相信马屁精的话。"

LXVI The Fox and the Crow

A Fox once saw a Crow **fly off**① with a piece of cheese in its **beak**② and settle on a branch of a tree. "That's for me, as I am a Fox," said Master Reynard, and he walked up to the foot of the tree. "Good day, Mistress Crow," he cried. "How well you are looking today: how **glossy**③ your feathers; how bright your eye. I feel sure your voice must **surpass**④ that of other birds, just as your figure does; let me hear but one song from you that I may greet you as the Queen of Birds."

The Crow lifted up her head and began to **caw**⑤ her best, but the moment she opened her mouth the piece of cheese fell to the ground, only to be snapped up by Master Fox. "That will do," said he. "That was all I wanted. In exchange for your cheese I will give you a piece of advice for the future: 'Do not trust **flatterers**⑥.'"

---

① fly off 飞离
② beak /biːk/ *n.* 鸟嘴
③ glossy /'glɔsi/ *a.* 光滑的,有光泽的
④ surpass /sɔ:'pɑːs/ *v.* 超越,胜过
⑤ caw /kɔː/ *v.* 乌鸦叫
⑥ flatterer /'flætərə/ *n.* 谄媚者,奉承者

六七　狐狸和葡萄

　　饥饿的狐狸看到几串熟透了的紫葡萄挂在高高的葡萄架上。她用尽了各种办法也够不到，只累得汗流浃背。最后，狐狸只好转身走开，她压抑着心头的失望，自言自语说：“这葡萄是酸的，没有我想的那么甜。”

LXVII　The Fox and the Grapes

　　A **Famished** ① Fox saw some **clusters** ② of **ripe** ③ black **grapes** ④ hanging from a **trellised** ⑤ **vine** ⑥. She **resorted** ⑦ to all her tricks to get at them, but wearied herself in vain, for she could not reach them. At last she turned away, hiding her disappointment and saying: "The Grapes are sour, and not ripe as I thought."

---

① famish /'fæmiʃ/ *v.* 使挨饿
② cluster /'klʌstə/ *n.* 串, 丛, 群
③ ripe /raip/ *a.* 成熟的
④ grape /greip/ *n.* 葡萄
⑤ trellis /'trelis/ *v.* 使(藤)在棚架上攀缘
⑥ vine /vain/ *n.* 攀爬植物, 藤, 蔓
⑦ resort /ri'zɔːt/ *v.* 求助于

六八　狐狸和豹子

狐狸和豹子争论谁更漂亮。豹子向狐狸炫耀他美丽斑斓的皮毛，但狐狸打断了他，对他说道："我可比你漂亮多了！我修饰的不是外表，而是头脑。"

LXVIII　The Fox and the Leopard

The Fox and the **Leopard**① **disputed**② which was the more beautiful of the two. The Leopard **exhibited**③ one by one the various spots which **decorated**④ his skin. But the Fox, interrupting him, said, "And how much more beautiful than you am I, who am decorated, not in body, but in mind."

---

① leopard /'lepəd/ n. 豹
② dispute /dis'pjuːt/ v. 争论
③ exhibit /ig'zibit/ v. 展现, 陈列
④ decorate /'dekəreit/ v. 装饰

六九　狐狸和面具

　　狐狸溜进一家剧院的储藏室，忽然发现一张脸正盯着自己，吓得大惊失色；他凑过去仔细一看，原来是一张演员戴的面具。狐狸叹道："哎，看起来挺漂亮，只可惜没长脑子。"

　　外表掩盖不了本质。

LXIX　The Fox and the Mask

A Fox had by some means got into the store-room of a **theater**①. Suddenly he **observed**② a face glaring down on him and began to be very frightened; but looking more closely he found it was only a Mask such as actors use to put over their face. "Ah," said the Fox, "you look very fine; it is a pity you have not got any brains."

Outside show is a poor **substitute**③ for inner worth.

---

① theater /ˈθiətə/ *n.* 剧场, 戏院
② observe /əbˈzəːv/ *v.* 注意到
③ substitute /ˈsʌbstitjuːt/ *n.* 代替者

七〇　狐狸和猴子

狐狸和猴子结伴旅行。路上，他们经过一处墓地，里面竖满了纪念碑。"所有你看到的这些纪念碑，"猴子对狐狸说，"都是纪念我的祖先的。他们在世的时候都是自由民和享有很高声望的公民。"狐狸答道："你撒谎的技术还真不赖，我相信你的祖先没一个会从墓里跳出来反驳你。"

谎言，经常会不攻自破。

LXX　The Fox and the Monkey

A Fox and a Monkey were traveling together on the same road. As they journeyed, they passed through a **cemetery**① full of **monuments**②. "All these monuments which you see," said the Monkey, "are erected in honor of my **ancestors**③, who were in their day freedmen and **citizens**④ of great renown." The Fox replied, "You have chosen a most appropriate subject for your **falsehoods**⑤, as I am sure none of your ancestors will be able to **contradict**⑥ you.

A false tale often **betrays**⑦ itself.

---

① cemetery /'semitri/ n. 公墓,墓地
② monument /'mɔnjumənt/ n. 纪念碑
③ ancestor /'ænsestə/ n. 祖宗,祖先
④ citizen /'sitizn/ n. 公民,市民
⑤ falsehood /fɔːlshud/ n. 谎言
⑥ contradict /kɔntrə'dikt/ v. 反驳
⑦ betray /bi'trei/ v. 出卖,背叛

七一 丢了尾巴的狐狸

有只狐狸误陷捕兽器，挣扎逃命时被夹断了尾巴。他深感羞辱，惶惶不可终日，就决意劝说所有的狐狸都相信，没有尾巴更漂亮，这样一来就能把自己的缺陷掩盖住了。他把很多只狐狸召集在一起，劝他们都割掉尾巴，说没了尾巴不仅看起来更优雅，而且也少了负担和累赘，再也不用刷尾巴了。一只狐狸插嘴说："朋友，要不是你自己没了尾巴，你就不会劝我们也把尾巴扔了。"

LXXI   The Fox Who Had Lost His Tail

A Fox caught in a trap escaped, but in so doing lost his tail. Thereafter, feeling his life a burden from the shame and **ridicule**① to which he was exposed, he schemed to **convince**② all the other Foxes that being **tailless**③ was much more **attractive**④, thus making up for his own **deprivation**⑤. He **assembled**⑥ a good many Foxes and publicly advised them to cut off their tails, saying that they would not only look much better without them, but that they would get rid of the weight of the brush, which was a very great **inconvenience**⑦. One of them interrupting him said, "If you had not yourself lost your tail, my friend, you would not thus **counsel**⑧ us."

---

① ridicule /'ridikjuːl/ *n.* 嘲笑，愚弄
② convince /kən'vins/ *v.* 说服，使……相信
③ tailless /'teillis/ *a.* 无尾巴的
④ attractive /ə'træktiv/ *a.* 有吸引力的
⑤ deprivation /ˌdepri'veiʃən/ *n.* 剥夺
⑥ assemble /ə'sembl/ *v.* 召集，聚集
⑦ inconvenience /inkən'viːniəns/ *n.* 不便，困难
⑧ counsel /'kaunsəl/ *v.* 劝告，建议

七二　青蛙和井

沼泽里住着两只青蛙。有一年夏天，天气非常炎热，沼泽里的水干涸了，喜欢潮湿环境的青蛙不得不去寻找一个新家。他们路过一口深井，一只青蛙向下看了看，对另一只说道："井底下看来很凉爽，我们不如就跳下去，住在这里吧。"另一只青蛙脑瓜比较聪明，答道："先别忙，我的朋友，要是这口井也像沼泽一样干了，我们怎么出来呢？"

遇事要三思而行。

LXXII　The Frogs and the Well

Two Frogs lived together in a **marsh**①. But one hot summer the marsh **dried up**②, and they left it to look for another place to live in: for frogs like **damp**③ places if they can get them. By and by they came to a deep well, and one of them looked down into it, and said to the other, "This looks a nice cool place. Let us jump in and settle here." But the other, who had a wiser head on his shoulders, replied, "Not so fast, my friend. Supposing this well dried up like the marsh, how should we get out again?"

Look before you leap.

---

① marsh /mɑːʃ/ *n.* 沼泽,湿地
② dry up 干涸
③ damp /dæmp/ *a.* 潮湿的

七三　蚊子和公牛

　　有只蚊子落在牛角上，在那儿待了很长时间。在飞走前，他嗡嗡地问公牛，是否希望他离开。牛答道："你来了，我不知道；你走了，我也不会想你。"

　　有些人总以为自己很重要，但别人却不以为意。

LXXIII　The Gnat and the Bull

　　A Gnat settled on the horn of a Bull, and sat there a long time. Just as he was about to fly off, he made a **buzzing**① noise, and inquired of the Bull if he would like him to go. The Bull replied, "I did not know you had come, and I shall not miss you when you go away."

　　Some men are of more **consequence**② in their own eyes than in the eyes of their neighbors.

---

① buzz /bʌz/ *v.* 作嗡嗡声
② consequence /'kɔnsikwəns/ *n.* 结果,后果

七四　山羊和牧羊人

　　牧羊人想把一只走失的山羊唤回羊群，他又吹口哨又吹号角，但掉队的山羊对此充耳不闻。后来，牧羊人拾起一块石头，向山羊扔去，不想一下子打断了羊角。牧羊人恳求山羊不要把这件事告诉他的主人，山羊回答说："你这个傻瓜，就算我不开口，羊角也会替我说话的。"

　　事实明摆着，掩人耳目也没用。

LXXIV　The Goat and the Goatherd

A **Goatherd**① had sought to bring back a stray goat to his flock. He **whistled** ② and sounded his horn in vain; the **straggler** ③ paid no attention to the summons. At last the Goatherd threw a stone, and breaking its horn, begged the Goat not to tell his master. The Goat replied, "Why, you **silly** ④ fellow, the horn will speak though I be silent."

Do not attempt to hide things which cannot be hid.

---

① goatherd /'ɡəuthə:d/ n. 牧羊人,牧羊者
② whistle /(h)wisl/ v. 吹口哨
③ straggler /'stræɡlə/ n. 游荡者,流浪者
④ silly /'sili/ a. 愚蠢的

七五　下金蛋的鹅

　　一天，农夫在鹅的窝里看到一枚黄澄澄的鹅蛋闪闪发光，他拾起来一掂，蛋竟然像铅一样沉甸甸的，农夫以为这是有人故意捉弄他，就想把蛋扔掉，但是转念一想，又把蛋带回了家。他把蛋仔仔细细地察看了一番，惊喜地发现这居然是一枚纯金的鹅蛋。从此，这只鹅每天早上都产下一枚金蛋，农夫靠卖金蛋，很快就发了大财。农夫的钱越多，他的心就变得越贪婪。他想一下子拿到所有的金蛋，于是就把鹅宰了，剖开鹅的肚子，却什么也没有找到。

　　贪婪的人经常被贪婪所害。

LXXV　The Goose with the Golden Eggs

One day a countryman going to the nest of his Goose found there an egg all yellow and glittering. When he took it up it was as heavy as lead and he was going to **throw it away**①, because he thought a trick had been played upon him. But he took it home on second thoughts, and soon found to his delight that it was an egg of pure gold. Every morning the same thing **occurred**②, and he soon became rich by selling his eggs. As he grew rich he grew greedy; and thinking to get at once all the gold the Goose could give, he killed it and opened it only to find nothing.

Greed often over reaches itself.

---

① throw away 扔掉
② occur /əˈkəː/ *v.* 发生

七六　野兔和狐狸

野兔和老鹰开战，请求狐狸来助阵。狐狸答道："如果我们不知道你们是谁，又不知道你们和谁交战，我们一定乐意挺身相助。"

许诺之前务必先计算得失。

LXXVI　The Hares and the Foxes

The Hares waged war with the Eagles, and called upon the Foxes to help them. They replied, "We would willingly have helped you, if we had not known who you were, and with whom you were fighting."

Count① the cost before you **commit**② yourselves.

---

① count /kaunt/ *v.* 计数
② commit /kə'mit/ *v.* 承诺

七七　野兔和猎狗

　　猎狗把野兔赶出了洞，在兔子后面紧紧追赶。跑了很长一段路之后，猎狗忽然停住脚步，不再追了。牧羊人看到猎狗停下来，就嘲弄他说："看来，还是那个小东西比你跑得快。"猎狗答道："你没有看到我们之间的区别——我跑是为了有饭吃，可他跑是为了逃命。"

LXXVII　The Hare and the Hound

　　A Hound started a Hare from his lair, but after a long run, gave up the **chase**①. A goatherd seeing him stop, **mocked**② him, saying "The little one is the best runner of the two." The Hound replied, "You do not see the difference between us: I was only running for a dinner, but he for his life."

① chase /tʃeis/ *n.* 追逐
② mock /mɔk/ *v.* 嘲弄

七八　野兔和狮子

野兔在动物集会上发表演说，提出所有动物应该一律平等。狮子答道："兔子啊，你说得不错，但你的话缺少像我们这样锋利的爪子和牙齿。"

LXXVIII　The Hares and the Lions

The Hares **harangued**① the **assembly**②, and argued that all should be equal. The Lions made this reply："Your words，O Hares！ Are good；but they lack both **claws**③ and teeth such as we have."

---

① harangue /həˈræŋ/ v. 长篇演说
② assembly /əˈsembli/ n. 集合，集会
③ claw /klɔː/ n. 爪

七九　龟兔赛跑

有一天，兔子嘲笑乌龟的短腿走得太慢，乌龟笑着答道："虽然你跑得像风一样快，但我可以在赛跑中赢你。"兔子认为乌龟的话实在是异想天开，就同意进行一场比赛，由狐狸来选定比赛路线和终点。到了比赛的那一天，龟兔同时冲出了起跑线。乌龟虽然走得慢，却是向着终点一刻不停地稳步前进；兔子半路上躺在路边呼呼大睡起来。等到兔子睡醒，飞快地接着向前跑时，却看见乌龟已经到达了终点，正舒舒服服地打盹呢。

锲而不舍就是胜利。

LXXIX　The Hare and the Tortoise

A Hare one day **ri diculed**① the short feet and slow pace of the Tortoise, who replied, laughing: "Though you be swift as the wind, I will beat you in a race." The Hare, believing her **assertion**② to be simply impossible, assented to the **proposal**③; and they agreed that the Fox should choose the course and fix the goal. On the day appointed for the race the two started together. The Tortoise never for a moment stopped, but went on with a slow but steady pace straight to the end of the course. The Hare, lying down by the wayside, fell fast asleep. At last waking up, and moving as fast as he could, he saw the **Tortoise**④ had reached the goal, and was comfortably dozing after her **fatigue**⑤.

Slow but steady wins the race.

---

① ridicule /'ridikju:l/ *v.* 嘲笑，嘲弄　　　　② assertion /ə'sə:ʃən/ *n.* 断言，主张
③ proposal /prə'pəuzəl/ *n.* 提议　　　　　　④ tortoise /'tɔ:təs/ *n.* 龟
⑤ fatigue /fə'ti:g/ *n.* 疲乏，疲劳

八〇　鹿和藤蔓

鹿为躲避猎人的追赶，藏到一大丛茂密的藤蔓底下。猎人们忙着向前追赶，没有注意到鹿的藏身之处。鹿以为平安无事了，就开始啃藤蔓上的嫩枝。有个猎人听到枝叶沙沙作响，回过头来看到了鹿，一箭就要了它的性命。垂死的鹿痛苦地呻吟着说："藤救了我的命，我却反过来吃它，如今送命，也是罪有应得。"

LXXX　The Hart and the Vine

A **Hart**①, hard pressed in the chase, hid himself beneath the large leaves of a Vine. The huntsmen, in their haste, overshot the place of his **concealment**②. Supposing all danger to have passed, the Hart began to **nibble**③ the **tendrils**④ of the Vine. One of the huntsmen, attracted by the rustling of the leaves, looked back, and seeing the Hart, shot an arrow from his bow and struck it. The Hart, at the point of death, groaned："I am rightly served, for I should not have **maltreated**⑤ the Vine that saved me."

---

① hart /haːt/ *n.* （五岁以上的）雄赤鹿
② concealment /kənˈsiːlmənt/ *n.* 隐匿，隐蔽，躲藏
③ nibble /ˈnibl/ *v.* 一点点地咬，慢慢啃
④ tendril /ˈtendril/ *n.* 卷须，蔓，卷须状之物
⑤ maltreat /mælˈtriːt/ *v.* 虐待

八一　鹿和猎人

鹿在池塘边喝水，看见自己俊美的身姿映在水里，心里非常得意，自言自语说："多美的鹿角啊，谁的角能像我这么高贵？可惜我的腿又细又轻，真希望它们也能长得体面些，配得上我头上的这顶王冠。"

正在这时，猎人过来了，他悄悄向鹿射了一箭，羽箭夹着风声呼啸而至。鹿一下子跳到一旁，躲开了这一箭，然后迈开敏捷的长腿，跑得几乎不见了踪影。可是当鹿跑过树林时，低垂的树枝缠住了他的鹿角，让鹿动弹不得，猎人趁机赶了上来。鹿不禁长叹一声："唉！我们常常轻视那些对我们最有用的东西。"

LXXXI The Hart and the Hunter

The Hart was once drinking from a pool and **admiring**① the noble figure he made there. "Ah," said he, "where can you see such noble horns as these, with such **antlers**②! I wish I had legs more worthy to bear such a noble crown; it is a pity they are so **slim**③ and slight."

At that moment a Hunter approached and sent an arrow whistling after him. Away bounded the Hart, and soon, by the aid of his **nimble**④ legs, was nearly out of sight of the Hunter; but not noticing where he was going, he passed under some trees with branches growing low down in which his antlers were caught, so that the Hunter had time to come up. "Alas! Alas!" cried the Hart: "We often **despise**⑤ what is most useful to us."

---

① admire /əd'maiə/ *v.* 钦佩，羡慕
② antler /'æntlə/ *n.* 鹿角，茸角
③ slim /slim/ *a.* 苗条的，细长的
④ nimble /'nimbl/ *a.* 敏捷的，伶俐的
⑤ despise /dis'paiz/ *v.* 轻视

八二　鹰、鸢和鸽子

鸽子见到鸢，感到很害怕，跑去求鹰来保护他们。鹰立刻就答应了。鸽子放鹰进鸽棚以后才发现，老鹰比鸢更可怕，他在一天之内吃掉的鸽子，比鸢一年抓走的都多。

切不可饮鸩止渴。

LXXXII　The Hawk, the Kite①, and the Pigeons

The Pigeons, terrified by the appearance of a Kite, called upon the Hawk to defend them. He at once **consented**②. When they had admitted him into the **cote**③, they found that he made more **havoc**④ and **slew**⑤ a larger number of them in one day than the Kite could pounce upon in a whole year.

Avoid a **remedy**⑥ that is worse than the disease.

---

① kite /kait/ *n.* 鸢
② consent /kən'sent/ *v.* 同意
③ cote /kəut/ *n.* 棚,窝,栏
④ havoc /'hævək/ *n.* 大破坏
⑤ slew /sluː/ *v.* (slay的过去式)杀害
⑥ remedy /'remidi/ *n.* 药物,治疗法

八三 母牛和公牛

母牛看到公牛套着挽具,辛苦地犁地,就嘲笑公牛命运不济,要被迫劳作。转眼到了收获季节,主人给公牛卸下牛轭,用绳子绑住母牛,牵到祭坛上去准备杀掉献祭。公牛见了,微笑着对母牛说道:"人们容得你游手好闲,是因为你马上就要被宰掉作祭品了。"

LXXXIII The Heifer and the Ox

A **Heifer**① saw an Ox hard at work harnessed to a **plow**②, and tormented him with reflections on his unhappy fate in being **compelled**③ to labor. Shortly afterwards, at the harvest festival, the owner released the Ox from his **yoke**④, but bound the Heifer with cords and led her away to the altar to be **slain**⑤ in honor of the occasion. The Ox saw what was being done, and said with a smile to the Heifer: "For this you were allowed to live in **idleness**⑥, because you were presently to be sacrificed."

---

① heifer /hefə/ *n.* 小母牛
② plow /plau/ *n.* 犁
③ compel /kəm'pel/ *v.* 强迫,迫使
④ yoke /jəuk/ *n.* 轭,轭状物
⑤ slain /slein/ *v.* (slay的过去分词)杀害
⑥ idleness /'aidlnis/ *n.* 懒惰,闲散

八四　母鸡和金蛋

　　农夫家里的母鸡每天下一枚金蛋。农夫和他的妻子认为母鸡肚子里一定藏着许多许多金蛋，为了拿到金子，他们杀死了母鸡，却惊奇地发现这只鸡同其他母鸡没有什么区别。这对傻瓜希望一夜暴富，到头来却葬送了原本每天都可以得到的钱财。

LXXXIV　The Hen and the Golden Eggs

　　A Cottager and his wife had a Hen that laid a golden egg every day. They supposed that the **Hen**[①] must contain a great **lump**[②] of gold in its inside, and in order to get the gold they killed it. Having done so, they found to their surprise that the Hen differed in no respect from their other hens. The foolish pair, thus hoping to become rich all at once, deprived themselves of the gain of which they were assured day by day.

---

① hen /hen/ *n.* 母鸡
② lump /lʌmp/ *n.* 很多

八五　赫拉克勒斯和马车夫

赶车人赶着马车走在乡村小路上，车轮忽然陷入了一道深沟，笨手笨脚的车夫被眼前的情况吓呆了，一动不动地望着马车，大声向大力神赫拉克勒斯求救。据说，赫拉克勒斯出现在马车夫面前，对他说："伙计，用你的肩膀顶住轮子，拿鞭子赶马！如果你还没有尽全力自救，就先别向我求救；要是光靠祈祷，你什么也得不到。"

自助是最好的帮助。

LXXXV　Hercules and the Wagoner

A **Carter**[①] was driving a **wagon**[②] along a country **lane**[③], when the wheels sank down deep into a **rut**[④]. The **rustic**[⑤] driver, stupefied and **aghast**[⑥], stood looking at the wagon, and did nothing but utter loud cries to Hercules to come and help him. Hercules, it is said, appeared and thus addressed him: "Put your shoulders to the wheels, my man. **Goad**[⑦] on your **bullocks**[⑧], and never more pray to me for help, until you have done your best to help yourself, or depend upon it you will **henceforth**[⑨] pray in vain."

Self-help is the best help.

---

① carter /'kɑːtə/ n. 运货马车夫
② wagon /'wægən/ n. 四轮马车，货车
③ lane /lein/ n. 小路，小巷
④ rut /rʌt/ n. 车辙，槽
⑤ rustic /'rʌstik/ a. 乡村的
⑥ aghast /ə'gɑːst/ a. 惊骇的，吓呆的
⑦ goad /gəud/ v. 用刺棒赶（牛），驱赶
⑧ bullock /'bulək/ n. 阉牛
⑨ henceforth /hens'fɔːθ/ ad. 今后

八六　马和驴 (版本一)

　　马配上漂亮的马鞍，趾高气扬地走在大路上，迎面来了一头驴，背上驮满了货物，慢吞吞地走着。马对驴说："我真忍不住要踢你一脚。"驴沉默不语，默默地恳求诸神主持公道。没过多久，马患上了气喘病，被主人卖给了一家牧场。驴看到马拉着粪车，就挖苦他说："喂，说大话的老兄，你那漂亮的马鞍子哪儿去了？不久以前你还瞧不起我，可现在你自己不是也沦落到这步田地了吗？"

LXXXVI　The Horse and the Ass

　　A Horse, proud of his fine **trappings**①, met an Ass on the highway. The Ass, being heavily laden, moved slowly out of the way. "Hardly," said the Horse, "can I resist kicking you with my heels." The Ass held his peace, and made only a silent **appeal**② to the justice of the gods. Not long afterwards the Horse, having become **broken-winded**③, was sent by his owner to the farm. The Ass, seeing him drawing a dungcart, thus **derided**④ him："Where, O **boaster**⑤, are now all thy gay trappings, thou who are thyself **reduced to**⑥ the condition you so lately treated with **contempt**⑦? "

---

① trapping /'træpiŋ/ *n.* 外部标志
② appeal /ə'pi:l/ *v.* 求助,诉请
③ broken-winded 喘气的
④ deride /di'raid/ *v.* 嘲笑,嘲弄
⑤ boaster /'bəustə/ *n.* 自夸的人
⑥ reduce to 降至
⑦ contempt /kən'tempt/ *n.* 轻视,轻蔑

八七　马和驴（版本二）

　　马和驴一起赶路，马配着漂亮的马鞍，一路上昂首阔步；驴背着重重的驮筐，艰难地前行。"我真希望自己是匹马，"驴一边叹气一边说，"吃得好，又不用干活，而且连挽具都这么好看。"第二天，爆发了激烈的战争，马在当天的最后一次冲锋中受了重伤，不治而亡。他的朋友，驴，恰巧经过战场，看着垂死的马，驴说道："我以前想错了，卑微的安全也强似荣耀的危险。"

LXXXVII　The Horse and the Ass

　　A Horse and an Ass were travelling together, the Horse **prancing**① along in its fine trappings, the Ass carrying with difficulty the heavy weight in its **panniers**②. "I wish I were you," sighed the Ass; "nothing to do and well fed, and all that fine harness upon you." Next day, however, there was a great battle, and the Horse was wounded to death in the final charge of the day. His friend, the Ass, happened to pass by shortly afterwards and found him on the point of death. "I was wrong," said the Ass: "Better **humble**③ security than **gilded**④ danger."

---

① prance /prɑːns/ v. 腾跃，欢跃，昂首阔步
② pannier /ˈpæniə/ n. 驮篮
③ humble /ˈhʌmbl/ a. 卑下的
④ gild /gild/ v. 镀金，虚饰

八八　马和马夫

马夫常常用一整天的时间给他的马梳理毛发，把马浑身上下擦拭得干干净净。但与此同时，他偷走了马的燕麦，卖了钱供自己花销。马说道："唉！要是你真心希望我过得好，不用整天梳来梳去，多给我一点饲料就行了。"

LXXXVIII　The Horse and Groom

A **Groom** ① used to spend whole days in **currycombing**② and rubbing down his Horse, but at the same time stole his **oats**③ and sold them for his own **profit**④. "Alas!" said the Horse, "if you really wish me to be in good condition, you should groom me less, and feed me more."

---

① groom /grum/ *n.* 马夫
② currycomb /ˈkʌriˌkəum/ *v.* 用马栉梳
③ oat /əut/ *n.* 燕麦
④ profit /ˈprɔfit/ *n.* 利益

八九　马和鹿

很久以前，马独占着大片平原，后来，鹿侵入了马的领地，分享他的草场。马决心报复这个外来者，就问一个人是否愿意帮他去教训一下鹿。这人回答说，如果马肯在嘴里咬一块嚼子，并且让他坐在马背上，他就会想出一条妙计来对付鹿。马同意了，让这人骑到了马背上。马发现，从那一刻起，自己不但没能向鹿报仇，反而沦为人的奴隶，供人驱使。

LXXXIX　The Horse and the Stag

At one time the Horse had the plain **entirely**① to himself. Then a Stag intruded into his **domain**② and shared his **pasture**③. The Horse, desiring to revenge himself on the stranger, asked a man if he were willing to help him in punishing the Stag. The man replied that if the Horse would receive a bit in his mouth and agree to carry him, he would **contrive**④ **effective**⑤ weapons against the Stag. The Horse consented and allowed the man to mount him. From that hour he found that instead of obtaining revenge on the Stag, he had **enslaved**⑥ himself to the service of man.

---

① entirely /in'taiəli/ *ad.* 完全地
② domain /dəu'mein/ *n.* 领域
③ pasture /'pɑːstʃə/ *n.* 牧场
④ contrive /kən'traiv/ *v.* 设计，图谋
⑤ effective /i'fektiv/ *a.* 有效的
⑥ enslave /in'sleiv/ *v.* 使做奴隶，使处于奴役的状态

九〇 马和骑兵

有个骑兵非常爱护他的战马。在战争期间，无论情况多么危急，他都把马视为自己的战友，用干草和谷子精心地喂养他。可是战争结束以后，他只给马吃谷糠，让他去驮沉重的木头，干各种繁重的劳役，还肆意地虐待他。

不久，战争的烽烟再起，号角声召唤骑兵归队，他给战马配上战时的装备，自己也身着沉重的铠甲，翻身上马。可他刚一坐上马背，马立刻就被压得趴倒在地，再也驮不动重担的马对他的主人说："你只能走着上战场了，你已经把我从一匹马变成了一头驴，你总不能指望我顷刻间又从驴变回马吧!"

XC   The Horse and His Rider

A Horse Soldier took the utmost pains with his charger. As long as the war lasted, he looked upon him as his fellow-helper in all **emergencies**① and fed him carefully with hay and corn. But when the war was over, he only allowed him **chaff**② to eat and made him carry heavy loads of wood, subjecting him to much **slavish**③ **drudgery**④ and **ill-treatment**⑤.

War was again **proclaimed**⑥, however, and when the **trumpet**⑦ summoned him to his standard, the Soldier put on his charger its military trappings, and **mounted**⑧, being **clad**⑨ in his heavy coat of **mail**⑩. The Horse fell down straightway under the weight, no longer equal to the burden, and said to his master, "You must now go to the war on foot, for you have **transformed**⑪ me from a Horse into an Ass; and how can you expect that I can again turn in a moment from an Ass to a Horse?"

---

① emergency /i'məːdʒnsi/ *n.* 紧急事件,紧急情况
② chaff /tʃɑːf/ *n.* 谷壳,糠
③ slavish /'sleiviʃ/ *a.* 奴隶的
④ drudgery /'drʌdʒəri/ *n.* 苦差事,苦工
⑤ ill-treatment 虐待
⑥ proclaim /prə'kleim/ *v.* 宣布,公告
⑦ trumpet /'trʌmpit/ *n.* 喇叭,喇叭声
⑧ mount /maunt/ *v.* 乘马
⑨ clad /klæd/ *v.* 穿衣,穿着
⑩ mail /meil/ *n.* 盔甲
⑪ transform /træns'fɔːm/ *v.* 转换

九一 猎人和伐木工

有个胆小的猎人在森林里搜寻狮子的踪迹，他问正在砍橡树的伐木工有没有见过狮子的脚印，知不知道狮子的巢穴在哪儿。伐木工说，"我这就带你去找狮子。"猎人听了，吓得脸色苍白，牙齿打战，哆哆嗦嗦地说："谢谢，不必了。我要找的是狮子的踪迹，不是狮子。"

语言和行动都勇敢才称得上英雄。

XCI　The Hunter and the Woodman

A Hunter, not very bold, was searching for the tracks of a Lion. He asked a man felling **oaks**① in the forest if he had seen any marks of his **footsteps**② or knew where his lair was. "I will," said the man, "at once show you the Lion himself." The Hunter, turning very pale and chattering with his teeth from fear, replied, "No, thank you. I did not ask that; it is his track only I am in search of, not the Lion himself."

The hero is brave in deeds as well as words.

---

① oak /əuk/ *n.* 橡树
② footstep /'futstep/ *n.* 脚步,足迹

九二　猎人和渔夫

猎人带着猎狗打猎归来，路上碰见了渔夫，他见渔夫拎着满满一篮子鱼，很羡慕，渔夫也对猎人袋中的猎物很有兴趣，于是两人立刻同意将各自一天的劳动成果做一个交换。这个安排让猎人和渔夫皆大欢喜，在接下来的一段日子里，他们每天都这样交换。最后，有位邻居对他们说："如果你们继续这样换下去，交换带来的乐趣很快就会因过于频繁而丧失殆尽，到那时，你们两人都会希望留住自己的猎物。"

节制带来乐趣。

XCII　The Huntsman and the Fisherman

A Huntsman, returning with his dogs from the field, fell in by chance with a Fisherman who was bringing home a basket well laden with fish. The Huntsman wished to have the fish, and their owner experienced an equal **longing**① for the contents of the game-bag. They quickly agreed to exchange the **produce**② of their day's sport. Each was so well pleased with his **bargain**③ that they made for some time the same exchange day after day. Finally a neighbor said to them, "If you go on in this way, you will soon destroy by frequent use the pleasure of your exchange, and each will again wish to **retain**④ the fruits of his own sport."

Abstain⑤ and enjoy.

---

① longing /'lɔŋiŋ/ *n.* 渴望
② produce /'prɔdjuːs/ *n.* 产品
③ bargain /'bɑːgin/ *n.* 协议，交易
④ retain /ri'tein/ *v.* 保持，保留
⑤ abstain /əb'stein/ *v.* 自制

九三　马、猎人和鹿

马和鹿之间起了争执，马跑去请猎人帮助他向鹿报仇。猎人同意了，但提出了几个条件："你要想打败鹿，就得让我把这块铁片放到你的嘴里，好让我用缰绳牵着你；还要让我把这个马鞍放到你的背上，好让我安安稳稳地坐在上面去追赶敌人。"马同意了，于是猎人很快给马配上了马鞍和缰绳。马有了猎人的帮助，没用多久就打败了鹿，他对猎人说："你现在可以下来了，把我嘴里和背上的东西统统拿走。"

"别着急，朋友，"猎人说，"我已经给你戴上了嚼子和马刺，我想让你从此就保持现在这副模样。"

如果你为了自己的目的让别人利用你，他们迟早也会为了自己的目的来利用你。

XCIII   The Horse, Hunter, and Stag

A quarrel had arisen between the Horse and the **Stag**①, so the Horse came to a Hunter to ask his help to take revenge on the Stag. The Hunter agreed, but said: "If you desire to conquer the Stag, you must permit me to place this piece of iron between your jaws, so that I may guide you with these **reins**②, and allow this **saddle**③ to be placed upon your back so that I may keep steady upon you as we follow after the enemy." The Horse agreed to the conditions, and the Hunter soon saddled and bridled him. Then with the aid of the Hunter the Horse soon overcame the Stag, and said to the Hunter: "Now, get off, and remove those things from my mouth and back."

"Not so fast, friend," said the Hunter. "I have now got you under bit and **spur**④, and prefer to keep you as you are at present."

If you allow men to use you for your own **purposes**⑤, they will use you for theirs.

---

① stag /stæg/ *n.* 牡鹿
② rein /rein/ *n.* 缰绳
③ saddle /'sædl/ *n.* 鞍
④ spur /'spəː/ *n.* 马刺
⑤ purpose /'pəːpəs/ *n.* 目的,意图

九四 墨丘利木像和木匠

有个木匠，人很穷，刻了一尊墨丘利木像，天天献祭，祈求发财。他千祈万求，可还是越来越穷。最后，他非常生气，就把木像从座上取下来，使劲地往墙上摔。木像的头摔了下来，从中流出一股金子；木匠赶快捡起来，说："啊，我想你凡事总是拧着来，真是不可理喻。敬你供你时，我得不到半点好处；现在扔你摔你，你倒给了我大笔财富。"

XCIV   The Image of Mercury and the Carpenter

A very poor man, a **Carpenter**① by trade, had a wooden image of Mercury, before which he made **offerings**② day by day, and begged the **idol**③ to make him rich, but in spite of his **entreaties**④ he became poorer and poorer. At last, being very angry, he took his image down from its **pedestal**⑤ and dashed it against the wall. When its head was knocked off, out came a stream of gold, which the Carpenter quickly picked up and said, "Well, I think thou art altogether **contradictory**⑥ and **unreasonable**⑦; for when I paid you honor, I reaped no benefits; but now that I maltreat you I am loaded with an **abundance**⑧ of riches."

---

① carpenter /'kɑːpintə/ *n.* 木匠　　② offering /'ɔfəriŋ/ *n.* 奉献物，牲礼
③ idol /'aidl/ *n.* 神像　　④ entreaty /in'triːti/ *n.* 恳求，哀求
⑤ pedestal /'pedistl/ *n.* 基架，座　　⑥ contradictory /ˌkɔntrə'diktəri/ *a.* 互相矛盾的
⑦ unreasonable /ʌn'riːznəbl/ *a.* 不合理的　　⑧ abundance /ə'bʌndəns/ *n.* 丰富，充裕

九五　寒鸦和鸽子

　　有只寒鸦，见鸽笼里几只鸽子食物丰盛，就把自己涂白，钻进去，分享鸽子丰富的食物。寒鸦不言，鸽子也就当他是一群的，让他进了鸽笼。

　　有一天，寒鸦忘乎所以，开始鸣叫，鸽子这才发现他的真面目，就赶他，用嘴啄他。寒鸦在鸽子中得不到食物，就返回寒鸦群里。寒鸦们见他一身白，也不认他，赶他，不让他跟他们在一起生活。寒鸦是两头都要得，两头都得不到。

XCV　The Jackdaw and the Doves

　　A **Jackdaw**①, seeing some Doves in a **cote**② abundantly provided with food, painted himself white and joined them in order to share their **plentiful** ③ **maintenance** ④. The Doves, as long as he was silent, supposed him to be one of themselves and admitted him to their cote.

　　But when one day he forgot himself and began to chatter, they discovered his true character and drove him forth, **pecking**⑤ him with their beaks. Failing to obtain food among the Doves, he returned to the Jackdaws. They too, not recognizing him on account of his color, expelled him from living with them. So desiring two ends, he obtained neither.

---

① jackdaw /ˈdʒækdɔː/ n. 寒鸦
② cote /kəut/ n. 棚，窝
③ plentiful /ˈplentiful/ a. 多的，丰富的
④ maintenance /ˈmeintinəns/ n. 生活费用
⑤ peck /pek/ v. 以喙啄

九六　寒鸦和狐狸

有只饿得半死的寒鸦立在一棵无花果树上，时令早已过了，树上仍结着几个果子。寒鸦等在那里，希望无花果会成熟。一只狐狸见他久立在那里，问明原因后，对他说，"先生，你这是在欺骗自己，真可悲；你抱着巨大的希望欺骗自己，但这希望带给你的只是欺蒙，绝不会给你带来欢乐。"

XCVI　The Jackdaw and the Fox

A Half-Famished Jackdaw seated himself on a **fig-tree**①, which had produced some fruit **entirely**② out of season, and waited in the hope that the figs would ripen. A Fox seeing him sitting so long and learning the reason of his doing so, said to him, "You are **indeed**③, sir, sadly deceiving yourself; you are **indulging**④ a hope strong enough to **cheat**⑤ you, but which will never **reward**⑥ you with enjoyment."

---

① fig-tree /fig tri:/【植】无花果树
② entirely /in'taiəli/ *ad.* 完全地
③ indeed /in'di:d/ *ad.* 的确，真正地
④ indulge /in'dʌldʒ/ *v.* 纵情于，放任
⑤ cheat /tʃi:t/ *v.* 欺骗
⑥ reward /ri'wɔ:d/ *v.* 奖赏；回报

九七　松鸦和孔雀

　　有只松鸦贸然走进孔雀常常盘桓的院子，发现了孔雀换羽时脱下的许多羽毛。松鸦把这些羽毛全绑在自己尾巴上，趾高气扬地向孔雀走去。他一走近，孔雀立刻发现是只假的，阔步走去啄他，啄去了他的假羽毛。松鸦不得已，只好回到松鸦群里。其他松鸦从远处旁观，也同样生他的气，对他说："高贵的鸟靠的不光是漂亮的羽毛。"

XCVII　The Jay and the Peacock

　　A Jay **venturing**① into a yard where **Peacocks**② used to walk, found there a number of feathers which had fallen from the Peacocks when they were **moulting**③. He tied them all to his tail and strutted down towards the Peacocks. When he came near them they soon discovered the cheat, and **striding**④ up to him pecked at him and plucked away his borrowed **plumes**⑤. So the Jay could do no better than go back to the other Jays, who had watched his behavior from a distance; but they were equally annoyed with him, and told him: "It is not only fine feathers that make fine birds."

---

① venture /'ventʃə/ v. 尝试，冒险一试
② peacock /'piːkɔk/ n. (雄)孔雀
③ moult /məult/ v. 换羽
④ stride /straid/ v. 迈大步走
⑤ plume /pluːm/ n. 羽毛

九八　朱庇特和猴子

朱庇特向林中百兽发布公告说，百兽中谁的幼子被公认为最英俊，谁就可以得到重赏。猴子与其他野兽一起前来，以母亲的万般柔情，推举一只丑陋、无毛、塌鼻子的小猴，去争夺这项大奖。听她介绍自己的儿子，大家直笑。她则坚定地说：“我不知朱庇特是否会把这奖颁发给我儿子，可有一点我确实知道，我是他的母亲，至少在我眼里他是最可爱、最英俊和最美丽的。”

XCVIII　Jupiter and the Monkey

Jupiter **issued**① a **proclamation**② to all the beasts of the forest and promised a royal reward to the one whose **offspring**③ should be deemed the **handsomest**④. The Monkey came with the rest and presented, with all a mother's tenderness, a flat-nosed, hairless, ill-featured young Monkey as a candidate for the promised reward. A general laugh **saluted**⑤ her on the presentation of her son. She resolutely said, "I know not whether Jupiter will **allot**⑥ the prize to my son, but this I do know, that he is at least in the eyes of me his mother, the dearest, handsomest, and most beautiful of all."

---

① issue /'isjuː/ *v.* 发出
② proclamation /prɔkləˈmeiʃn/ *n.* 宣言，公布
③ offspring /'ɔfspriŋ/ *n.* 子孙，后代
④ handsome /'hænsəm/ *a.* 英俊的
⑤ salute /səˈluːt/ *v.* 行礼，致意
⑥ allot /əˈlɔt/ *v.* 分配

九九　小羊和狼

有只小羊从草原归来，没有护卫，遭到狼的追逐。眼看无法脱身，小羊就转过身来说道："我知道，狼友，我注定要成为你口中之物。不过死前，我有个请求，请你给我弹奏一曲，让我跳个舞。"狼同意了，就吹奏起来，小羊跳着，几只猎狗听见了，跑来追赶狼。狼转过身，对小羊说："我这是自作自受；我原本只是个屠夫，不该吹奏曲子来让你开心。"

身陷绝境之时，关键是要有智谋。

IC　The Kid and the Wolf

A Kid, returning without protection from the **pasture**①, was pursued by a Wolf. Seeing he could not escape, he turned round, and said:"I know, friend Wolf, that I must be your prey, but before I die I would ask of you one favor—you will play me a **tune**② to which I may dance." The Wolf **complied**③, and while he was **piping**④ and the Kid was dancing, some hounds hearing the sound ran up and began chasing the Wolf. Turning to the Kid, he said, "It is just what I deserve; for I, who am only a **butcher**⑤, should not have turned piper to please you."

In time of **dire**⑥ need, clever thinking is key.

---

① pasture /'pɑːstʃə/ n. 牧场
② tune /tjuːn/ n. 歌曲
③ comply /kəm'plai/ v. 答应
④ pipe /paip/ v. 吹奏管乐
⑤ butcher /'butʃə/ n. 屠夫
⑥ dire /'daiə/ a. 极端的

一〇〇　鸢和天鹅

古时候，鸢和天鹅都有特殊的歌唱天赋。可是听到骏马嘶鸣后，他们非常着迷，试图模仿。模仿马叫时，却忘了如何歌唱。

希求假想的好处，常常会失去现有的福分。

C　The Kites and the Swans

The Kites of olden times, as well as the **Swans**①, had the **privilege**② of song. But having heard the neigh of the horse, they were so **enchanted**③ with the sound, that they tried to imitate it; and, in trying to neigh, they forgot how to sing.

The desire for imaginary benefits often **involves**④ the loss of present blessings.

① swan /swɔn/ *n.* 天鹅
② privilege /'privilidʒ/ *n.* 特权
③ enchant /in't ʃɑːnt/ *v.* 使……迷惑
④ involve /in'vɔlv/ *v.* 涉及

一〇一　羔羊和狼

狼追羔羊，羔羊逃往一座神庙里求救。狼大声对他叫道："祭司要是抓住了你，会把你杀了献祭的。"羔羊答道："我宁愿做神庙里的牺牲，也不愿给你吃掉。"

CI　The Lamb and the Wolf

A Wolf pursued a Lamb, which fled for refuge to a certain Temple. The Wolf called out to him and said, "The **Priest**① will **slay**② you in **sacrifice**③, if he should catch you." On which the Lamb replied, "It would be better for me to be sacrificed in the Temple than to be eaten by you."

---

① priest /priːst/ *n.* 教士,神父,祭司
② slay /slei/ *v.* 杀,杀害,残杀
③ sacrifice /ˈsækrifais/ *n.* 牺牲

一〇二　国王的儿子与狮子的画像

有个国王，生了个独子，喜欢舞枪弄棒。国王做了一个梦，梦见儿子会给狮子杀死。国王怕此梦成真，就给儿子造了座可爱的宫殿，墙上装饰着各种逼真的动物画像，好让儿子开心，其中有一幅就是狮子的画像。

年轻的王子看到这幅画像，突然为自己被这么关起来感到悲哀。他站在狮子近旁，说："噢，你这最可恶的动物！我父亲做了一个荒唐的梦，在梦中看到了你；就因为你，我被关在这里，好像我是个女孩子；我现在拿你怎么办？"说完，他伸出双手，去攀一棵棘刺树，想折下一根树枝作棍子，来打那狮子。可是他的手指给树刺扎破了，非常痛，发了炎，一阵晕眩，就倒下了。他突然一阵高烧，没过多少天就死了。

遇到困难烦恼，与其逃避，不如勇敢面对。

CII The King's Son and the Painted Lion

A King, whose only son was fond of **martial**① exercises, had a dream in which he was warned that his son would be killed by a lion. Afraid the dream should prove true, he built for his son a pleasant palace and **adorned**② its walls for his amusement with all kinds of life-sized animals, among which was the picture of a lion.

When the young Prince saw this, his grief at being thus **confined**③ burst out afresh, and, standing near the lion, he said: "O you most detestable of animals! Through a lying dream of my father's, which he saw in his sleep, I am shut up on your account in this palace as if I had been a girl; what shall I now do to you?" With these words he stretched out his hands toward a thorn-tree, meaning to cut a stick from its branches so that he might beat the lion. But one of the tree's **prickles**④ pierced his finger and caused great pain and **inflammation**⑤, so that the young Prince fell down in a fainting **fit**⑥. A violent **fever**⑦ suddenly set in, from which he died not many days later.

We had better bear our troubles bravely than try to escape them.

---

① martial /'mɑːʃəl/ a. 军事的,战争的
② adorn /ə'dɔːn/ v. 装饰
③ confine /kən'fain/ v. 限制,闭居
④ prickle /'prikl/ n. (动物或植物上的)刺,棘
⑤ inflammation /inflə'meiʃən/ n. 发炎,红肿
⑥ fit /fit/ n. (疾病等的)突然发作
⑦ fever /'fiːvə/ n. 发烧

一〇三　农夫和蛇

　　一条蛇，紧靠一个农舍的门口挖了洞，狠狠地咬了农舍主人的幼子一口。儿子死了，父亲很痛心，决意要把蛇杀了。第二天，蛇出洞觅食，他就拿起斧头去砍，但砍得太急，没砍中头，只砍下了尾巴梢。

　　不久后，农夫怕蛇也会咬自己，就极力讲和，在蛇洞里放了一些面包和盐。蛇发出轻轻的嘶嘶声，说："从今以后，我们不会和平相处了；我一看到你，就会想起自己失去的尾巴；你一看到我，就会想到自己死去的儿子。"

　　在施害者面前，受害者不会真正忘记自己所受的伤害。

CIII The Laborer and the Snake

A Snake, having made his hole close to the **porch**① of a **cottage**②, **inflicted**③ a mortal bite on the Cottager's **infant**④ son. Grieving over his loss, the Father resolved to kill the Snake. The next day, when it came out of its hole for food, he took up his axe, but by **swinging**⑤ too hastily, missed its head and cut off only the end of its tail.

After some time the Cottager, afraid that the Snake would bite him also, endeavored to make peace, and placed some bread and salt in the hole. The Snake, slightly **hissing**⑥, said: "There can henceforth be no peace between us; for whenever I see you I shall remember the loss of my tail, and whenever you see me you will be thinking of the death of your son."

No one truly forgets **injuries**⑦ in the presence of him who caused the injury.

---

① porch /pɔːtʃ/ *n.* 门廊
② cottage /'kɔtidʒ/ *n.* 村舍,小屋
③ inflict /in'flikt/ *v.* 施以,加害
④ infant /'infənt/ *n.* 婴儿,幼儿
⑤ swing /swiŋ/ *v.* 摇摆,使……旋转
⑥ hiss /his/ *v.* 发出嘘声,发嘶嘶声
⑦ injury /'indʒəri/ *n.* 损害,伤害

一〇四　灯

一盏灯注的油太多，非常明亮，就吹嘘自己比太阳还亮。突然起了一阵风，一下把灯吹灭了。灯的主人又把灯点亮，说："别再瞎吹了，今后静静发光就是了。要知道，就是小星星也不需要重新点燃。"

CIV　The Lamp

A Lamp，**soaked**① with too much oil and **flaring**② brightly, boasted that it gave more light than the sun. Then a sudden **puff**③ of wind arose，and the Lamp was immediately **extinguished**④. Its owner lit it again，and said："Boast no more, but **henceforth**⑤ be content to give thy light in silence. Know that not even the stars need to be relit."

---

① soak /səuk/ *v.* 浸，吸入
② flaring /'flɛəriŋ/ *a.* 火焰摇曳的，过分艳丽的
③ puff /pʌf/ *n.* (风的)吹，呼(之声)
④ extinguish /iks'tiŋgwiʃ/ *v.* 熄灭
⑤ henceforth /hens'fɔːθ/ *ad.* 今后

一〇五　云雀葬父

古话说，大地未开辟之时，就有了云雀。云雀的父亲死时，因没有大地，所以找不到埋葬父亲的地方。她让父亲停尸五天；到了第六天，实在别无他法，就把父亲葬在自己的头脑里。因此，她长出了一个冠，人们都说那是她父亲的坟丘。

年轻人的首要责任是孝敬父母。

CV　The Lark Burying Her Father

The **Lark**①, according to an ancient legend, was created before the earth itself, and when her father died, as there was no earth, she could find no place of burial for him. She let him lie **uninterred**② for five days, and on the sixth day, not knowing what else to do, she buried him in her own head. Hence she obtained her **crest**③, which is popularly said to be her father's grave-hillock.

Youth's first duty is **reverence**④ to parents.

---

① lark /lɑːk/ *n.* 云雀
② inter /in'tə:/ *v.* 埋葬
③ crest /krest/ *n.* 冠
④ reverence /'revərəns/ *n.* 敬畏，尊敬

一〇六　狮子和鹰

有只鹰停下，请狮子与他结成互利联盟。狮子答道："我没意见。不过，请原谅，我要请你保证你言而有信，因为朋友虽然立了约，可只要他乐意，随时都可以一飞了之，教我如何信任他？"

试过了再相信。

CVI　The Lion and the Eagle

An Eagle stayed his flight and entreated a Lion to make an **alliance**① with him to their **mutual**② advantage. The Lion replied, "I have no **objection**③, but you must excuse me for requiring you to find surety for your good faith, for how can I trust anyone as a friend who is able to fly away from his bargain whenever he pleases?"

Try before you trust.

---

① alliance /ə'laiəns/ *n.* 联盟
② mutual /'mjuːtjuəl/ *a.* 共同的,相互的
③ objection /əb'dʒekʃən/ *n.* 反对,异议

一〇七　狮子和野兔

狮子碰见了一只酣睡的野兔，正要去抓她，蓦然看见一只漂亮的年轻公鹿慢慢跑过，撂下兔子就去追公鹿。兔子被追赶声吓醒，拔腿就跑。狮子追了老远没有追上公鹿，回来要吃兔子，发现兔子也跑了，他说："我真是活该，放弃了到手的食物，去追逐更大的诱惑。"

CVII　The Lion and the Hare

A Lion came across a Hare, who was fast asleep. He was just in the act of seizing her, when a fine young Hart **trotted**[①] by, and he left the Hare to follow him. The Hare, scared by the noise, awoke and scudded away. The Lion was unable after a long chase to catch the Hart, and returned to feed upon the Hare. On finding that the Hare also had **run off**[②], he said, "I am rightly served, for having let go of the food that I had in my hand for the chance of obtaining more."

---

① trot /trɔt/ v. 快步走
② run off 离开

一〇八　狮子和老鼠

狮子在酣睡，有只老鼠从他脸上跑过，把他弄醒了。狮子大怒，起身抓住老鼠，要杀死他，可老鼠哀求道："你只要饶了我的性命，我定会报答你的大恩大德。"狮子笑笑，放了他。不久以后，狮子给猎人抓住了，被他们用结实的绳子捆在地上。老鼠听出了狮子的吼声，过来用牙咬断了绳子，放了狮子，然后高声道：

"我说我能帮你，你可以指望我报答你的好意，你当初听了直乐。现在你知道了吧，即使是老鼠，也能给狮子带来好处。"

CVIII　The Lion and the Mouse

A Lion was awakened from sleep by a Mouse **running over**[①] his face. Rising up angrily, he caught him and was about to kill him, when the Mouse **piteously**[②] entreated, saying: "If you would only **spare**[③] my life, I would be sure to repay your kindness." The Lion laughed and let him go. It happened shortly after this that the Lion was caught by some hunters, who bound him by strong **ropes**[④] to the ground. The Mouse, recognizing his roar, came **gnawed**[⑤] the rope with his teeth, and set him free, exclaimed:

"You ridiculed the idea of my ever being able to help you, expecting to receive from me any repayment of your favor. Now you know that it is possible for even a Mouse to **confer**[⑥] benefits on a Lion."

---

① run over 从……上面过去
② piteously /'pitiəsli/ *ad.* 可怜地, 凄惨地
③ spare /speə/ *v.* 饶恕, 不伤害
④ rope /rəup/ *n.* 绳, 索
⑤ gnaw /nɔː/ *v.* 咬
⑥ confer /kən'fəː/ *v.* 给予

一〇九　狮子和雕像

有个人和狮子讨论人和狮子谁更有力量。人说，他的伙伴和他更聪明，因而也更有力量。"跟我来，"他叫道，"我很快就可证明我说的没错。"于是他领着狮子来到公园里，给狮子看一尊赫拉克勒斯的雕像：赫拉克勒斯制服一只狮子，把狮子的嘴撕成了两半。

"这很好，"狮子说，"不过证明不了什么，因为这尊雕像是人塑的。"

我们希望事物是什么样，就容易把事物描绘成什么样。

CIX　The Lion and the Statue

A Man and a Lion were discussing the relative strength of men and lions **in general**①. The Man contended that he and his fellows were stronger than lions by reason of their greater **intelligence**②. "Come now with me," he cried, "and I will soon prove that I am right." So he took him into the public gardens and showed him a statue of Hercules overcoming the Lion and tearing his mouth in two.

"That is all very well," said the Lion, "but proves nothing, for it was a man who made the statue."

We can easily **represent**③ things as we wish them to be.

---

① in general 一般,通常,一般说来
② intelligence /in'telidʒəns/ n. 理解力,智力
③ represent /ˌrepri'zent/ v. 表现,描绘

一一〇　狮子和三只公牛

有三只公牛长时间在一块吃草。一头狮子埋伏一旁，想猎捕公牛，可见他们老在一块，又不敢出击。最后，狮子用花言巧语把公牛分开，等他们单独吃草时，就毫不畏惧地袭击他们，然后不慌不忙地把公牛逐个吃掉。

团结就是力量。

CX　The Lion and the Three Bulls

Three Bulls for a long time **pastured**① together. A Lion lay in **ambush**② in the hope of making them his prey, but was afraid to attack them while they kept together. Having at last by **guileful**③ speeches succeeded in separating them, he attacked them without fear as they fed alone, and feasted on them one by one at his own leisure.

Union is strength.

---

① pasture /'pɑːstʃə/ *v.* 吃草
② ambush /'æmbuʃ/ *n.* 埋伏，伏兵
③ guileful /'gailful/ *a.* 狡猾的，狡黠的

一一一　狮子、老鼠和狐狸

夏日酷热，有头狮子疲惫不堪，就在洞中酣然睡去。有只老鼠从他的鬃鬣和耳朵上跑过，把他弄醒了。狮子站起来，大怒，抖抖身子，到处搜寻那只老鼠。一只狐狸看见了，就说："你真是个了不起的狮子，怕老鼠。"

"我不是怕老鼠，"狮子说，"是老鼠这般放肆无礼令我生气。"

小处失礼，大招人忌。

CXI　The Lion, the Mouse, and the Fox

A Lion, fatigued by the heat of a summer's day, fell fast asleep in his **den**①. A Mouse ran over his mane and ears and woke him from his **slumbers**②. He rose up and shook himself in great wrath, and searched every corner of his den to find the Mouse. A Fox seeing him said: "A fine Lion you are, to be frightened of a Mouse."

"It's not the Mouse I fear," said the Lion, "I resent his **familiarity**③ and ill-breeding."

Little **liberties**④ are great **offenses**⑤.

---

① den /den/ *n.* 兽穴，洞穴
② slumber /'slʌmbə/ *n.* 睡眠
③ familiarity /fə,mili'æriti/ *n.* 随便，放肆
④ liberty /'libəti/ *n.* 自由
⑤ offense /ə'fens/ *n.* 冒犯

一一二　坠入爱河的狮子

狮子爱上了一个美丽的少女，就向她父母求婚。二位老人不知说什么。他们不想把女儿许给狮子，可也不愿惹怒百兽之王。最后，父亲说："阁下求婚，我们深感荣幸。可你明白，我们的女儿还年幼，怕你一时动情，会伤了她。我可否冒昧建议阁下，除了你的爪，拔了你的牙，然后我们再好好地考虑你的求婚。"

狮子爱得死去活来，于是就削了自己的爪，拔了自己的大牙。可等狮子再回来找少女的父母求婚时，他们当着狮子的面只是笑，就是不同意，让狮子有本事尽管使出来好了。

爱可以让最狂野者驯服。

CXII   The Lion in Love

A Lion once fell in love with a beautiful maiden and proposed marriage to her parents. The old people did not know what to say. They did not like to give their daughter to the Lion, yet they did not wish to **enrage**① the King of Beasts. At last the father said: "We feel highly honored by your Majesty's **proposal**②, but you see our daughter is a tender young thing, and we fear that in the **vehemence**③ of your affection you might possibly do her some injury. Might I **venture**④ to suggest that your Majesty should have your claws removed, and your teeth **extracted**⑤, then we would gladly consider your proposal again."

The Lion was so much in love that he had his claws trimmed and his big teeth taken out. But when he came again to the parents of the young girl they simply laughed in his face, and bade him do his worst.

Love can **tame**⑥ the wildest.

---

① enrage /in'reidʒ/ v. 激怒，使暴怒
② proposal /prə'pəuzəl/ n. 求婚
③ vehemence /'viːiməns/ n. 热烈
④ venture /'ventʃə/ v. 尝试，冒险一试
⑤ extract /iks'trækt/ v. 拔掉
⑥ tame /teim/ v. 使……驯服

一一三　狮子、熊和狐狸

　　狮子和熊同时抓住了一只小羊，二者为争夺小羊打得不可开交。他们彼此狠撕猛咬，久斗不止，力气渐衰，终于累得倒在地上。

　　有只狐狸，远远地绕着他们转了几圈，看到他们都躺在地上，小羊卧在他们中间安然无恙。于是，狐狸跑过去，抓住小羊，飞奔而去。狮子和熊看见了，可是没有力气，站不起来，"我们打来打去，累得要死，结果却便宜了狐狸，活该倒霉。"

　　有时候，一人全任其劳，他人尽得其利。

CXIII   The Lion, the Bear, and the Fox

A Lion and a Bear seized a Kid at the same moment, and fought fiercely for its **possession**①. When they had fearfully **lacerated**② each other and were faint from the long combat, they lay down **exhausted**③ with **fatigue**④.

A Fox, who had gone round them at a distance several times, saw them both stretched on the ground with the Kid lying untouched in the middle. He ran in between them, and seizing the Kid **scampered**⑤ off as fast as he could. The Lion and the Bear saw him, but not being able to get up, said, "Woe be to us, that we should have fought and belabored ourselves only to serve the turn of a Fox."

It sometimes happens that one man has all the **toil**⑥, and another all the profit.

① possession /pə'zeʃən/ *n.* 拥有
② lacerate /'læsəreit/ *v.* 撕裂，伤害
③ exhausted /ig'zɔːstid/ *a.* 筋疲力尽的
④ fatigue /fə'tiːg/ *n.* 疲乏
⑤ scamper /'skæmpə/ *v.* 奔跑，快跑
⑥ toil /tɔil/ *n.* 辛苦

一一四 狮子、狐狸和驴

狮子、狐狸和驴订下合约，狩猎时要互相协助。他们在森林里抓到了一个大猎物，回来后，狮子要驴按合约给他们仨各分一份。驴小心翼翼地把猎物分成三等份，恭请狮子和狐狸先挑。狮子勃然大怒，将驴吞食了。然后，他请狐狸辛苦一下，来分一分。狐狸把猎物堆成一大堆，只给自己留了少而又少的一小口。

狮子道："我的好伙伴，这种分法是谁教你的？你得那一份正好。"狐狸答道："我亲眼看见了驴的命运，是从驴那里学来的。"

从别人的不幸中汲取教训的人是幸福的。

CXIV   The Lion, the Fox, and the Ass

The Lion, the Fox and the Ass entered into an agreement to assist each other in the chase. Having secured a large **booty**[1], the Lion on their return from the forest asked the Ass to allot his due portion to each of the three partners in the treaty. The Ass carefully divided the spoil into three equal shares and **modestly**[2] requested the two others to make the first choice. The Lion, bursting out into a great rage, devoured the Ass. Then he requested the Fox to do him the favor to make a division. The Fox **accumulated**[3] all that they had killed into one large heap and left to himself the smallest possible **morsel**[4].

The Lion said, "Who has taught you, my very excellent fellow, the art of division? You are perfect to a **fraction**[5]." He replied, "I learned it from the Ass, by witnessing his fate."

Happy is the man who learns from the misfortunes of others.

---

[1] booty /'buːti/ n. 战利品

[2] modestly /'mɔdistli/ ad. 谦逊地

[3] accumulate /ə'kjuːmjuleit/ v. 积聚,堆积

[4] morsel /'mɔːsəl/ n. 一口,少量,一片

[5] fraction /'frækʃən/ n. 小部分

一一五　狮子、狐狸和野兽

狮子宣布，他大病将死，召百兽前来听他的遗嘱。山羊来到了狮子洞中，在里面听了很久。接着有只绵羊走了进去。绵羊还没出来，一只牛犊又来接受百兽之王的最后祝愿。可是狮子似乎很快就康复了，他来到洞口，看见已在外面等了一阵子的狐狸。

"你为什么不来问候我？"狮子对狐狸说。

"求阁下海涵。"狐狸道，"不过，我查看了已到你这里来的动物的足迹，但见许多进去的蹄印，不见一个出来。进洞的动物出来之前，我想先待在外面。"

落入敌人的陷阱易，逃出敌人的陷阱难。

CXV The Lion, the Fox, and the Beasts

The Lion once gave out that he was sick unto death and summoned the animals to come and hear his last **Will**① and **Testament**②. So the Goat came to the Lion's cave, and stopped there listening for a long time. Then a Sheep went in, and before she came out a Calf came up to receive the last wishes of the Lord of the Beasts. But soon the Lion seemed to recover, and came to the mouth of his cave, and saw the Fox, who had been waiting outside for some time.

"Why do you not come to pay your respects to me?" said the Lion to the Fox.

"I beg your Majesty's pardon," said the Fox, "but I noticed the track of the animals that have already come to you; and while I see many hoof-marks going in, I see none coming out. Till the animals that have entered your cave come out again I **prefer to**③ remain in the open air."

It is easier to get into the enemy's toils than out again.

---

① will /wil/ *n.* 遗嘱
② testament /'testəmənt/ *n.* 确实证明
③ prefer to 更喜欢(宁愿)

一一六　母狮子

原野上百兽在争论，谁应得到一胎下崽最多的最高荣誉。他们吵吵嚷嚷冲到母狮子面前，要求她做出裁判。"你，"百兽说，"你一胎生多少个幼狮?"母狮嘲笑他们，说："啊! 我只生一个，可这一个却是不折不扣的纯种狮子。"

价值在于质，不在于量。

CXVI　The Lioness

A **controversy**① **prevailed**② among the beasts of the field as to which of the animals deserved the most credit for producing the greatest number of whelps at a birth. They rushed **clamorously**③ into the presence of the Lioness and demanded of her the **settlement**④ of the **dispute**⑤. "And you," they said, "how many sons have you at a birth?" The Lioness laughed at them, and said: "Why! I have only one; but that one is altogether a **thoroughbred**⑥ Lion."

The value is in the worth, not in the number.

---

① controversy /'kɔntrəvəːsi/ *n.* 争论，争议
② prevail /pri'veil/ *v.* 盛行，流行
③ clamorously /'klæmərəsli/ *ad.* 吵闹地
④ settlement /'setlmənt/ *n.* 解决
⑤ dispute /dis'pjuːt/ *n.* 争论
⑥ thoroughbred /'θʌrəbred/ *a.* 纯种的

一一七　小男孩和命运女神

　　有个小男孩长途跋涉，累坏了，就在一口深井的沿上躺了下来。据说，小男孩差一点掉进井水中，命运女神出现在他面前，把他从睡梦中唤醒；她对小男孩说道："小男孩，请醒一醒：你要是掉进井里，人们会责怪我，我就要在人间担骂名；因为我发现，人因过失招了灾祸，不论自己实际上有多少不是，肯定会怪我。"

　　每个人都可不同程度地主宰自己的命运。

CXVII　The Little Boy and Fortune

A little boy wearied with a long journey, lay down overcome with fatigue on the very **brink**① of a deep well. Being within an inch of falling into the water, Dame Fortune, it is said, appeared to him, and waking him from his **slumber**②, thus addressed him: "Little boy, pray wake up: for had you fallen into the well, the blame will be thrown on me, and I shall get an ill name among mortals; for I find that men are sure to blame their **calamities**③ to me, however much by their own **folly**④ they have really brought them on themselves."

Every one is more or less master of his own fate.

---

① brink /briŋk/ *n.* 边缘
② slumber /'slʌmbə/ *n.* 睡眠
③ calamity /kə'læmiti/ *n.* 灾难，不幸事件
④ folly /'fɔli/ *n.* 愚蠢的行为

一一八　狮子的份额

有一次，狮子跟狐狸、豺狗和狼一块去打猎。他们不停追赶，终于对一只成年牡鹿发起突然攻击，很快就将牡鹿杀死了。接着就是如何分猎物的问题。"把这只牡鹿给我分成四份。"狮子吼道，于是其他三个动物就剥了牡鹿的皮，把牡鹿分成四份。狮子站在鹿尸前，宣布了他的意见："第一份归我，因为我是百兽之王；第二份归我，因为我是仲裁者；另一份也归我，因为我也参与了狩猎；至于第四份，啊，至于这一份，我看你们谁敢动它一爪子。"

"哼。"狐狸咕哝着，夹着尾巴走开了；不过他咕哝的声音很小。

你可以与强者共苦，却无法与强者同甘。

CXVIII   The Lion's Share

The Lion went once a hunting along with the Fox, the Jackal, and the Wolf. They hunted and they hunted till at last they surprised a Stag, and soon took its life. Then came the question how the spoil should be divided. "Quarter me this Stag," roared the Lion; so the other animals skinned it and cut it into four parts. Then the Lion took his stand in front of the **carcass**① and **pronounced**② judgment: "The first quarter is for me in my **capacity**③ as King of Beasts; the second is mine as **arbiter**④; another share comes to me for my part in the chase; and as for the fourth quarter, well, as for that, I should like to see which of you will dare to lay a paw upon it."

"Humph," **grumbled**⑤ the Fox as he walked away with his tail between his legs; but he spoke in a low **growl**⑥.

You may share the labors of the great, but you will not share the **spoil**⑦.

---

① carcass /ˈkɑːkəs/ n. (动物的)尸体
② pronounce /prəˈnauns/ v. 宣告
③ capacity /kəˈpæsiti/ n. 能力
④ arbiter /ˈɑːbitə/ n. 仲裁人
⑤ grumble /ˈɡrʌmbl/ v. 嘟囔
⑥ growl /ɡraul/ n. 低声威胁
⑦ spoil /spɔil/ n. 战利品

一一九　男人和两个心上人

　　有位中年人，头发已开始发白。他同时追求两个女人。一个年轻，另一个年纪已经很大了。年长的女人觉得被比自己小的男人追求，难堪，所以她打定主意，追求者一来，就拔掉他一撮黑发。相反，年轻的女人不想嫁给一个老头，所以也同样热心地拔掉她能找到的每一根白发。结果，周旋在她们俩人中间，他很快就发现自己头上一根头发也不剩了。

　　欲讨人人欢，反遭人人怨。

CXIX　The Man and His Two Sweethearts

　　A middle-aged man, whose hair had begun to turn **gray**①, **courted**② two women at the same time. One of them was young, and the other well advanced in years. The elder woman, ashamed to be courted by a man younger than herself, made a point, whenever her admirer visited her, to pull out some portion of his black hairs. The younger, on the contrary, not wishing to become the wife of an old man, was equally **zealous**③ in removing every gray hair she could find. Thus it came to pass that between them both he very soon found that he had not a hair left on his head.

　　Those who seek to please everybody please nobody.

---

① gray /grei/ *a.* 灰色的
② court /kɔːt/ *v.* 献殷勤，追求
③ zealous /'zeləs/ *a.* 热心的，积极的

一二〇　男人和两个妻子

从前，允许男人多妻，有个中年男人娶了两个妻子，一老一少。二人都很爱他，希望看到他像自己。此时，这个男人已开始有白发了，少妻不喜欢，因为白发衬得他太老了，与自己不般配。所以，每天晚上，少妻给他梳头，都把白发拔掉。老妻见他有了白发非常开心，因为她不愿给人误当作他的妈妈。所以，每天早上，老妻给他梳理头发，见了黑发，能拔多少就拔多少。结果，这个男人很快就发现自己全秃了。

事事迁就，很快就无事可以迁就了。

CXX　The Man and His Two Wives

In the old days, when men were allowed to have many wives, a middle-aged Man had one wife that was old and one that was young; each loved him very much, and desired to see him like herself. Now the Man's hair was turning gray, which the young Wife did not like, as it made him look too old for her husband. So every night she used to comb his hair and pick out the white ones. But the elder Wife saw her husband growing gray with great pleasure, for she did not like to be mistaken for his mother. So every morning she used to arrange his hair and pick out as many of the black ones as she could. The consequence was the Man soon found himself entirely bald.

Yield① to all and you will soon have nothing to yield.

---

① yield /ji:ld/ *v.* 屈服

一二一　丢失的假鬃

　　有头可笑的老狮子，不幸鬣鬃都掉光了。一天，风很大，他外出散步，就戴上了假鬃。

　　狮子一抬头，发现街对面有一只迷人的虎妹子。为引起对方的注意，他淡然一笑，鞠了一个优美的躬。正在这时，突然刮来一阵强风，把他的假鬃吹掉了，他晾在那里，觉得傻乎乎的，显得更尴尬，光秃秃的脑袋像弹子一样熠熠生光。狮子起初有点难堪，可接着对虎小姐微微一笑，道："我自己的毛发都不愿待在我的头上，别人的不肯待在那儿，有什么可奇怪的？"

　　风趣的人总是应对自如。

CXXI   The Lost Wig

A funny old Lion, who had the misfortune to lose his **mane**[1], was wearing a **wig**[2] as he was taking a **stroll**[3] on a very windy day.

Looking up, he spied one of the charming Tiger sisters across the street, and, wishing to make an impression, smiled **blandly**[4] and made a beautiful low bow. At that moment a very smart gust of wind came up, and the consequence was that his wig **flew off**[5] and left him there, feeling foolish and looking worse, with his bald head **glistening**[6] like a **billiard**[7] ball. Though somewhat **embarrassed**[8] at first, he smiled at the Lady and said: "Is it a wonder that another fellow's hair shouldn't keep on my head, when my own wouldn't stay there?"

Wit[9] always has an answer ready.

---

① mane /mein/ *n.* (马等的)鬃毛
② wig /wig/ *n.* 假发
③ stroll /strəul/ *n.* 闲逛, 漫步
④ blandly /'blændli/ *ad.* 温和地, 柔和地, 殷勤地
⑤ fly off 飞走
⑥ glisten /glisn/ *v.* 闪亮
⑦ billiard /'biljəd/ *a.* 撞球的
⑧ embarrassed /im'bærəst/ *a.* 尴尬的, 局促不安的
⑨ wit /wit/ *n.* 智力, 才智

一二二 男人和妻子

有个男人娶了个妻子，家里人人不待见。他想知道妻子是否也同样招娘家人嫌，就找个借口打发她回娘家探亲。

不久妻子回来了，他就问她过得怎么样，仆人待她如何。妻子回答道："放牛的、放羊的都向我投来厌恶的眼神。"

他说，"噢，老婆，如果连早出晚归的牧人都不喜欢你，那么整天和你在一起的人又该做何感想！"

看草知风向。

CXXII The Man and His Wife

A Man had a Wife who made herself hated by all the members of his household. Wishing to find out if she had the same effect on the persons in her father's house, he made some **excuse**① to send her home on a visit to her father.

After a short time she returned, and when he inquired how she had got on and how the servants had treated her, she replied, "The herdsmen and shepherds **cast on**② me looks of aversion."

He said, "O Wife, if you were disliked by those who go out early in the morning with their **flocks**③ and return late in the evening, what must have been felt towards you by those with whom you passed the whole day! "

Straws show how the wind **blows**④.

---

① excuse /iks'kju:z/ *n.* 借口，理由　　② cast on 向某一方向传递
③ flock /flɔk/ *n.* 一群(牛、羊等)　　④ blow /bləu/ *n.* 吹

一二三 人和狮子

有个人与狮子一块穿越森林。他们很快就开始吹嘘自己比对方有力，比对方勇敢。他们争着争着，经过一尊石像，那石像雕的是"人扼死的狮子"。

行人指着石像说："瞧那儿！瞧我们人多强壮，是如何战胜百兽之王的。"狮子答道："这石像是你们人雕的。如果我们狮子懂得如何塑雕像，你就会看到人被踩在狮子的利爪下。"

故事一个比一个精彩。

CXXIII The Man and the Lion

A Man and a Lion traveled together through the forest. They soon began to boast of their respective **superiority**① to each other in strength and **prowess**②. As they were disputing, they passed a **statue**③ carved in stone, which represented "a Lion **strangled**④ by a Man."

The traveler pointed to it and said: "See there! How strong we are, and how we prevail over even the king of beasts." The Lion replied: "This statue was made by one of you men. If we Lions knew how to **erect**⑤ statues, you would see the Man placed under the paw of the Lion."

One story is good, till another is told.

---

① superiority /sjupiəri'ɔriti/ *n.* 优越性,优势
② prowess /'prauis/ *n.* 英勇,勇猛
③ statue /'stætjuː/ *n.* 塑像,雕像
④ strangle /'stræŋgl/ *v.* 勒死,使窒息
⑤ erect /i'rekt/ *v.* 建造

一二四　男人和萨提儿

有个男人和森林之神萨提儿曾同饮为盟。隆冬的一天，他们一块说话，男人把手指放在嘴上吹。萨提儿问他为什么这样，男人告诉萨提儿，他的手冰凉，呵气暖一暖。后来，他们坐下来吃饭，饭很烫。男人把一盘菜稍稍凑近嘴边，往里面吹气。萨提儿又问为什么，他说肉太烫了，吹吹让它凉一凉。

"我不能再把你当朋友了，"萨提儿说，"因为你这种人，同是吹气，又吹热又吹凉。"

CXXIV　The Man and the Satyr

A Man and a Satyr once drank together in **token**① of a bond of alliance being formed between them. one very cold **wintry**② day，as they talked，the Man put his fingers to his mouth and blew on them. When the Satyr asked the reason for this，he told him that he did it to warm his hands because they were so cold. Later on in the day they sat down to eat，and the food prepared was quite **scalding**③. The Man raised one of the dishes a little towards his mouth and blew in it. When the Satyr again inquired the reason，he said that he did it to cool the meat，which was too hot.

"I can no longer consider you as a friend，" said the Satyr，"a fellow who with the same breath blows hot and cold."

---

① token /ˈtəukən/ *n.* 表征
② wintry /ˈwintri/ *a.* 冬天的
③ scalding /ˈskɔ:ldiŋ/ *a.* 滚烫的

一二五　猴子和骆驼

　　林中百兽举行一次盛大的演出，猴子站起来跳舞。他逗得观众大乐，赢得一片掌声，然后坐了下来。骆驼羡慕猴子得到大家赞赏，也想博得宾客的喜爱，轮到他时也提出要站起来给大家跳个舞。骆驼扭来扭去，极为荒唐，百兽一阵愤怒，都拿棒子打他，将他赶出了兽群。

　　见好的，切忌乱模仿。

CXXV　The Monkey and the Camel

　　The Beasts of the forest gave a splendid entertainment at which the Monkey stood up and danced. Having **vastly**① delighted the **assembly**②, he sat down **amidst**③ universal **applause**④. The Camel, envious of the praises bestowed on the Monkey and desiring to **divert to**⑤ himself the favor of the guests, proposed to stand up in his turn and dance for their **amusement**⑥. He moved about in so utterly ridiculous a manner that the Beasts, in a fit of **indignation**⑦, set upon him with clubs and drove him out of the assembly.

　　It is **absurd**⑧ to **ape**⑨ our betters.

---

① vastly /ˈvɑːstli/ *ad.* 极大地
② assembly /əˈsembli/ *n.* 集合，集会
③ amidst /əˈmidst/ *prep.* 在……当中
④ applause /əˈplɔːz/ *n.* 鼓掌，喝彩
⑤ divert to 使……转向
⑥ amusement /əˈmjuːzmənt/ *n.* 娱乐，消遣
⑦ indignation /ˌindigˈneiʃən/ *n.* 愤怒
⑧ absurd /əbˈsəːd/ *a.* 荒唐的
⑨ ape /eip/ *v.* 模仿

一二六　人和蛇

有个乡下人的儿子偶然踩着了蛇，蛇掉头咬了他一口，他就死了。父亲大怒，操起斧子去追蛇，把蛇的尾巴砍掉了一节。蛇图谋报复，咬了农夫的几头牛，给他造成了严重损失。农夫觉得最好与蛇和解，于是就拿着食物和蜜来到蛇洞口，对蛇说：

"让我们忘掉旧恶吧，也许你惩罚我儿子，伤害我的家畜没错，可我要为儿子报仇肯定也是应该的。既然我们都如愿了，为什么不再做朋友呢？"

"不，不成，"蛇说，"拿走你的礼物吧。你绝不可能忘掉死去的儿子，我也不会忘记自己丢了尾巴。"

伤害也许可以原谅，但不会被忘记。

CXXVI   The Man and the Serpent

A Countryman's son by accident trod upon a Serpent's tail, which turned and bit him so that he died. The father **in a rage**[①] got his **axe**[②], and pursuing the Serpent, cut off part of its tail. So the Serpent in revenge began stinging several of the Farmer's cattle and caused him severe loss. Well, the Farmer thought it best to make it up with the Serpent, and brought food and honey to the mouth of its lair, and said to it:

"Let's forget and forgive; perhaps you were right to punish my son, and take vengeance on my cattle, but surely I was right in trying to revenge him; now that we are both satisfied why should not we be friends again?"

"No, no," said the Serpent, "take away your gifts; you can never forget the death of your son, nor I the loss of my tail."

Injuries may be forgiven, but not forgotten.

①　in a rage 一怒之下
②　axe /æks/ n. 斧

一二七　猴子和猴妈妈

据说，猴子一胎生两个小猴，爱一个恨一个。猴妈妈对一个是精心抚养，对另一个却不管不问。但备受疼爱的小猴因猴妈妈过分疼爱被闷死了，而遭到嫌弃的小猴，虽然没人疼爱，却顺利长大。

打算再周密也难保万无一失。

CXXVII　The Monkeys and Their Mother

The Monkeys, it is said, has two young ones at each birth. The Mother **fondles**① one and **nurtures**② it with the greatest affection and care, but hates and neglects the other. It happened once that the young one which was caressed and loved was smothered by the too great affection of the Mother, while the despised one was nurtured and **reared**③ in spite of the neglect to which it was **exposed**.④

The best **intentions**⑤ will not always ensure success.

---

① fondle /'fɔndl/ *v.* 爱，爱抚，溺爱
② nurture /'nəːtʃə/ *v.* 养育
③ rear /riə/ *v.* 养育
④ expose /iks'pəuz/ *v.* 暴露，显露
⑤ intention /in'tenʃən/ *n.* 意图，目的

一二八 大山分娩

一座大山一次非常狂躁。呻吟、喧嚷之声震耳，人群从四面八方涌来，看个究竟。他们聚集在一起，焦虑地等待着可怕的灾难发生，结果生出来一只老鼠。

千万不要小题大做。

CXXVIII The Mountain in Labor

A Mountain was once greatly **agitated**①. Loud groans and noises were heard, and crowds of people came from all parts to see what was the matter. While they were assembled in anxious expectation of some terrible **calamity**②, out came a Mouse.

Don't make much **ado**③ about nothing.

---

① agitate /'ædʒiteit/ v. 使……摇动，骚动
② calamity /kə'læmiti/ n. 灾难，不幸事件
③ ado /ə'du:/ n. 忙乱，无谓的纷扰

一二九　北风和太阳

北风和太阳争论谁最强大，并说定谁先让行人脱下衣服，就宣布谁是胜者。北风先发威，他使尽全力，可风刮得越猛，行人的大衣裹得越紧。最后，北风放弃了取胜的希望，要求太阳来试，看太阳有何能耐。太阳突然光芒四射，和煦至极。行人感受到太阳温暖的光芒，马上就把衣服一件一件地脱下来，最后实在热得没法，就脱光了衣服，到路边小溪中洗了个澡。

说服胜过强迫。

CXXIX　The North Wind and the Sun

The North Wind and the Sun disputed as to which was the most powerful, and agreed that he should be **declared**[1] the victor who could first **strip**[2] a **wayfaring**[3] man of his clothes. The North Wind first tried his power and blew with all his might, but the keener his **blasts**[4], the closer the Traveler wrapped his cloak around him, until at last, resigning all hope of victory, the Wind called upon the Sun to see what he could do. The Sun suddenly shone out with all his warmth. The Traveler no sooner felt his **genial**[5] **rays**[6] than he took off one garment after another, and at last, fairly overcome with heat, undressed and bathed in a stream that lay in his path.

Persuasion[7] is better than Force.

---

① declare /di'klɛə/ *v.* 宣布
② strip /strip/ *v.* 脱衣
③ wayfare /'weifɛə/ *v.* 旅行（尤指步行）
④ blast /blɑ:st/ *n.* 强烈的气流
⑤ genial /dʒi'naiəl/ *a.* 温和的，温暖的
⑥ ray /rei/ *n.* 光线
⑦ persuasion /pə'sweiʒən/ *n.* 说服

一三〇 橡树和芦苇

有一棵很大的橡树，被风拔起，刮到小溪对面，落在芦苇丛中。它就对芦苇说道："我真不明白，你们这么轻这么弱，强风竟然丝毫也没有把你们摧折。"芦苇回答说："你与风抗争，所以被摧毁了；可我们则相反，一有风吹，就赶紧弯伏，因此没有给摧折。"

屈以求伸。

CXXX The Oak and the Reeds

A very large Oak was **uprooted**① by the wind and thrown across a stream. It fell among some Reeds, which it **thus**② addressed: "I wonder how you, who are so light and weak, are not entirely crushed by these strong winds." They replied, "You fight and contend with the wind, and consequently you are destroyed; while we **on the contrary**③ bend before the least breath of air, and therefore remain unbroken, and escape."

Stoop④ to conquer.

---

① uproot /ʌp'ruːt/ v. 连根拔起

② thus /ðʌs/ ad. 如此，这样，因此，从而

③ on the contrary 正相反

④ stoop /stuːp/ v. 弯下，屈服

一三一　橡树和樵夫

樵夫砍倒了一棵山橡树，用树枝做楔子，把树干劈开。橡树叹道："根遭斧子砍伐我不介意，可被自己的树枝削成的楔子劈碎却着实让我伤心。"

自己造成的不幸最难忍受。

CXXXI　The Oak and the Woodcutter

The Woodcutter cut down a Mountain Oak and **split**[①] it in pieces, making **wedges**[②] of its own branches for dividing the trunk. The Oak said with a sigh, "I do not care about the blows of the axe aimed at my roots, but I do **grieve**[③] at being torn in pieces by these wedges made from my own branches."

Misfortunes **springing from**[④] ourselves are the hardest to bear.

---

① split /split/ *v.* 劈开
② wedge /wedʒ/ *n.* 楔子；楔形物
③ grieve /griːv/ *v.* 感到悲痛
④ spring from 起源于

一三二　老人和死神

有个老樵夫，劳作一生已腰弯背驼。他在林中捡柴，最后实在太累，感到绝望了，就把柴捆撂下来，大声叫道："这种生活我再也受不了啦。啊，但愿死神降临，把我收去。"

他正说着，死神，一具可怕的骷髅，出现了，对他说："喂，你有什么事？我听见你叫我。"

"先生，"樵夫答道，"你能否行个好，帮我个忙，把这捆柴火放在我肩上？"

真要如愿以偿，我们经常会遗憾的。

CXXXII　The Old Man and Death

An old **laborer**[1], **bent**[2] double with age and toil, was gathering sticks in a forest. At last he grew so tired and hopeless that he threw down the bundle of sticks, and cried out: "I cannot bear this life any longer. Ah, I wish Death would only come and take me!"

As he spoke, Death, a **grisly**[3] **skeleton**[4], appeared and said to him: "What wouldst thou, Mortal? I heard thee call me."

"Please, sir," replied the woodcutter, "would you kindly help me to lift this faggot of sticks on to my shoulder?"

We would often be sorry if our wishes were **gratified**[5].

---

① laborer /'leibərə/ n. 工人（劳动者）　② bent /bent/ a. 弯曲的
③ grisly /'grizli/ a. 恐怖的，可怕的　④ skeleton /'skelitən/ n. 骨架
⑤ gratify /'grætifai/ v. 使满足

一三三 老妪和酒坛

有个老妪找到一个空酒坛，不久前还装满了上等陈酒，此时仍留有酒香。她用鼻子贪婪地在酒坛上嗅着，嗅了一回又一回，说："多香醇啊! 留在坛子里的酒味都这么甘醇芳香，那酒该多么香呀!"

善行永留在人们的记忆中。

CXXXIII The Old Woman and the Wine Jar

An Old Woman found an empty jar which had lately been full of **prime**① old wine and which still retained the fragrant smell of its former contents. She greedily placed it several times to her nose, and drawing it backwards and forwards said, "O most **delicious**②! How nice must the wine itself have been, when it leaves behind in the very **vessel**③ which contained it so sweet a **perfume**④! "

The memory of a good **deed**⑤ lives.

---

① prime /praim/ *a.* 最好的

② delicious /di'liʃəs/ *a.* 可口的, 美味的

③ vessel /'vesl/ *n.* 容器

④ perfume /'pəːfjuːm/ *n.* 香气, 芳香

⑤ deed /diːd/ *n.* 事迹, 行为

一三四　牛和青蛙

牛在水塘边饮水，踩着了一窝小青蛙，一只小青蛙被踩死了。青蛙妈妈来了，见少了个孩子，就问青蛙兄弟怎么回事。"他死了，亲爱的妈妈；刚才，一个巨兽，长着四个大蹄子，来到水塘边饮水，用后蹄把他踩死了。"青蛙妈妈吸气鼓腹，问道："那动物是不是这么大个儿。"

"妈妈，别再鼓气了，"她的儿子说道，"也别生气了。那怪物非常庞大，我敢肯定，你还没学像，自己的肚子就先鼓破了。"

CXXXIV　The Ox and the Frog

An Ox drinking at a pool trod on a **brood**① of young frogs and crushed one of them to death. The Mother coming up, and missing one of her sons, inquired of his brothers what had become of him. "He is dead, dear Mother; for just now a very huge beast with four great feet came to the pool and crushed him to death with his **cloven**② heel."

The Frog, puffing herself out, inquired, "if the beast was as big as that in size."

"**Cease**③, Mother, to puff yourself out," said her son, "and do not be angry: for you would, I assure you, sooner burst than successfully imitate the hugeness of that monster."

---

① brood /bruːd/ *n.* 窝
② cloven /'kləuvn/ *a.* 偶蹄的
③ cease /siːs/ *v.* 停止

一三五　牛和车轴

　　牛拉着一辆沉重的大车走在乡间小路上，车轴嘎吱山响。牛听见了，回头对车轮说道："嗨！你们干吗这么吵呀？活都教我们干了，该叫的不是你们，而是我们。"

　　受累最多的叫得最少。

CXXXV　The Oxen and the Axle-Trees

　　A heavy wagon was being dragged along a country lane by a team of Oxen. The Axle-Trees groaned and **creaked** [①] terribly; whereupon the Oxen, turning round, thus addressed the wheels: "Hello there! Why do you make so much noise? We bear all the labor, and we, not you, ought to cry out."

　　Those who suffer most cry out the least.

---

① creak /kriːk/ *v.* 作碾轧声,发出碾轧声

一三六 牛和屠夫

从前，牛想法要毁了屠夫，因为屠夫干的这一行是毁灭牛类。为了达到目的，一天，群牛聚在一处，把角磨利，要决一雌雄。可有一头牛，犁过许多地，已老态龙钟，他说道："不错，这些屠夫是屠宰我们牛类，可他们手法娴熟，没有造成不必要的痛苦。如果我们除掉了他们，我们就会落入生手手中，会死得加倍痛苦。你们不用怀疑，即便屠夫都死光了，人也绝不能缺少牛肉。"

切不可匆匆行事，当心换来另一种灾难。

CXXXVI The Oxen and the Butchers

The Oxen once upon a time sought to destroy the Butchers, who practiced a trade destructive to their race. They assembled on a certain day to carry out their purpose, and sharpened their horns for the **contest**①. But one of them who was **exceedingly**② old （for many a field had he plowed） thus spoke: "These Butchers, it is true, slaughter us, but they do so with skillful hands, and with no unnecessary pain. If we get rid of them, we shall fall into the hands of unskillful **operators**③, and thus suffer a double death: for you may be assured, that though all the Butchers should perish, yet will men never want beef."

Do not be in a hurry to change one evil for another.

---

① contest /'kɔntest/ n. 斗争
② exceedingly /ik'si:diŋli/ ad. 极其，极度地
③ operator /'ɔpəreitə/ n. 操作员

一三七　山鹬和猎人

有个捕猎野禽的人抓住了一只山鹬，要把他杀了。山鹬恳求猎人饶命，他说："求你了，老爷，别杀我，我会引来许多山鹬，以报答你的大恩大德。"

猎人答道，"现在我杀你更心安理得了，因为你为了保住自己的小命，不惜出卖你的亲戚和朋友。"

CXXXVII　The Partridge and the Fowler

A **Fowler**① caught a **Partridge**② and was about to kill him. The Partridge earnestly begged him to spare his life, saying, "Pray, master, permit me to live and I will **entice**③ many Partridges to you in **recompense**④ for your mercy to me."

The Fowler replied, "I shall now with less **scruple**⑤ take your life, because you are willing to save it at the cost of betraying your friends and relations."

---

① fowler /'faulə/ *n.* 捕鸟者
② partridge /'pɑːtridʒ/ *n.* 鹧鸪
③ entice /in'tais/ *v.* 诱骗，引诱
④ recompense /'rekəmpəns/ *n.* 酬谢，报答
⑤ scruple /'skruːpl/ *n.* 顾忌，迟疑

一三八　孔雀和鹤

有只开屏的孔雀讥讽从旁边经过的鹤，嘲笑鹤灰不溜丢的羽毛。孔雀说：“我像国王一样，佩金饰，着紫袍，绚丽似彩虹；而你翅膀上却没有一点颜色。”

“不错。”鹤答道，“不过我能直冲云霄，对星辰放声歌唱，可你却像公鸡，在粪堆上的鸟群里走来走去。”

羽毛漂亮，鸟未必好。

CXXXVIII　The Peacock and the Crane

A Peacock spreading its **gorgeous**① tail mocked a **Crane**② that passed by, ridiculing the **ashen**③ hue of its plumage and saying, "I am robed, like a king, in gold and purple and all the colors of the rainbow; while you have not a bit of color on your wings."

"True," replied the Crane; "but I soar to the heights of heaven and lift up my voice to the stars, while you walk below, like a cock, among the birds of the **dunghill**④."

Fine feathers don't make fine birds.

---

① gorgeous /ˈgɔːdʒəs/ a. 华丽的，美丽的
② crane /krein/ n. 鹤
③ ashen /ˈæʃən/ a. 灰色的，苍白的
④ dunghill /ˈdʌnhil/ n. 粪堆，堆肥

一三九　孔雀和朱诺

　　有一次，孔雀祈求女神朱诺，希望除了自己的其他动人之处外，也能拥有夜莺一样甜美的歌喉，朱诺拒绝了他的要求。孔雀仍不罢休，并指出自己是她心爱的鸟，朱诺说："乐天知命吧，人不能事事第一。"

CXXXIX　The Peacock and Juno

A Peacock once placed a **petition**① before Juno desiring to have the voice of a **nightingale**② in addition to his other attractions; but Juno refused his request. When he persisted, and pointed out that he was her favorite bird, she said: "Be content with your lot; one cannot be first in everything."

---

① petition /pi'tiʃən/ *n.* 祈求
② nightingale /'naitiŋgeil/ *n.* 夜莺

一四〇 顽皮的驴

一只驴爬上屋顶，在上面蹦蹦跳跳，把瓦片踢得粉碎。主人连忙追上去，把驴轰下来，用一根粗木棒把驴痛打一顿。驴说道："昨天，我看见猴子做同样的事，你们个个哈哈大笑，就好像看到非常好玩的事一样。"

CXL The Playful Ass

An Ass **climbed**① up to the roof of a building, and **frisking**② about there, broke in the **tiling**③. The  owner went up after him and quickly drove him down, beating him severely with a thick wooden **cudgel**④. The Ass said, "Why, I saw the Monkey do this very thing yesterday, and you all laughed heartily, as if it afforded you very great **amusement**⑤."

---

① climb /klaim/ *v.* 攀登
② frisk /'frisk/ *v.* 胡乱跑跳
③ tiling /'tailiŋ/ *n.* 盖瓦
④ cudgel /'kʌdʒəl/ *n.* 短棍，棒
⑤ amusement /ə'mju:zmənt/ *n.* 娱乐，消遣

一四一 石榴树、苹果树和荆棘

石榴树和苹果树争论谁最美。他们争得最凶时，邻近篱笆的一丛荆棘提高嗓门，以自吹自擂的口气说道："我亲爱的朋友，至少在我面前，请不要再做这种无谓的争论了。"

CXLI The Pomegranate, Apple-Tree, and Bramble

The **Pomegranate**① and Apple-Tree disputed as to which was the most beautiful. When their strife was at its height, a **Bramble**② from the neighboring hedge lifted up its voice, and said in a boastful tone: "Pray, my dear friends, in my presence at least cease from such vain disputings."

---

① pomegranate /ˈpɔmgrænit/ *n.* 石榴
② bramble /ˈbræmbəl/ *n.* 荆棘

一四二　预言家

有位术士坐在集市上，给过路的行人算命，突然有一人飞奔而来，对术士通报说，他的房门给撬开了，有人正在偷他的东西。他深深叹了一口气，就匆匆离去，跑得要多快有多快。一位邻居看见他在跑，就说道："喂！这位伙计！你说你能预测他人的祸福，怎么没有预见到自己的呀？"

CXLII　The Prophet

A **Wizard**①, sitting in the marketplace, was telling the fortunes of the passers-by when a person ran up in great haste, and announced to him that the doors of his house had been broken open and that all his goods were being stolen. He sighed heavily and hastened away as fast as he could run. A neighbor saw him running and said, "Oh!　You fellow there!　You say you can **foretell**② the fortunes of others; how is it you did not foresee your own?"

---

① wizard /'wizəd/ *n.* 男巫，术士
② foretell /fɔː'tel/ *v.* 预言，预测

一四三　渡鸦和天鹅

渡鸦看到一只天鹅，就想自己也有天鹅那般美丽的羽毛。他以为天鹅洁白无比，是因为常在水中游，给水洗的，所以就离开了附近常去觅食的祭坛，住到了湖中和池塘里。渡鸦一有时间就洗濯自己的羽毛，可就是无法改变羽毛的颜色。他因为缺乏食物而饿死了。

习惯可改，本性难移。

CXLIII　The Raven and the Swan

A **Raven**[1] saw a Swan and desired to secure for himself the same beautiful plumage. Supposing that the Swan's splendid white color arose from his washing in the water in which he swam, the Raven left the altars in the neighborhood where he picked up his living, and took up residence in the lakes and pools. But cleansing his feathers as often as he would, he could not change their color, while through want of food he **perished**[2].

Change of habit cannot **alter**[3] nature.

---

① raven /'reivən/ *n.* 渡鸦
② perish /'periʃ/ *v.* 毁灭，死亡
③ alter /'ɔːltə/ *v.* 改变

一四四　富人和皮匠

有个富人和皮匠比邻而居，因无法忍受鞣皮场中难闻的气味，就迫使这位邻居搬走。皮匠一次又一次推迟，老说就要离开了，可仍然不搬。时间久了，富人也就习惯了那难闻的气味，觉得没什么妨碍，也就不再抱怨了。

CXLIV　The Rich Man and the Tanner

A Rich Man lived near a **Tanner**①, and not being able to **bear**② the unpleasant smell of the tan-yard, he pressed his neighbor to go away. The Tanner put off his departure from time to time, saying that he would leave soon. But as he still continued to stay, as time went on, the rich man became accustomed to the smell, and feeling no **manner**③ of inconvenience, made no further **complaints**④.

---

① tanner /'tænə/ n. 制革工人
② bear /beə/ v. 忍受
③ manner /'mænə/ n. 方式
④ complaint /kəm'pleint/ n. 抱怨

一四五　河与海

　　河流联合起来向大海抱怨："我们注入大海时原本甘甜可口，都是因为你，我们才变得又咸又苦，这是为什么？"大海心里明白，河流是想把全部责任都推给自己，于是说道："请你们不要再流到我这里来，你们也就不会再变咸了。"

CXLV　The Rivers and the Sea

　　The Rivers joined together to complain to the Sea, saying, "Why is it that when we flow into your tides so **potable**① and sweet, you work in us such a change, and make us salty and unfit to drink?" The Sea, **perceiving**② that they intended to throw the blame on him, said, "Pray cease to flow into me, and then you will not be made **briny**③."

---

① potable /'pəutəbl/ *a.* 适于饮用的
② perceive /pə'si:v/ *v.* 察觉
③ briny /'braini/ *a.* 咸的

一四六　玫瑰和不凋花

玫瑰和不凋花在园中并肩开放，不凋花对邻居说："你又美丽，又芬芳，我多羡慕你呀！难怪你到处受欢迎。"

可玫瑰带着一丝忧伤回答道："啊，我亲爱的朋友，我只花开一时，我的花瓣很快就会枯萎凋零，然后我也就死去了。可你的花，即使折下来，也不会褪色，因为它们是永不凋谢的。"

非凡自有非凡的苦恼。

CXLVI　The Rose and the Amaranth

A Rose and an **Amaranth**① **blossomed**② side by side in a garden, and the Amaranth said to her neighbor, "How I envy you your beauty and your sweet **scent**③! No wonder you are such a **universal**④ favorite."

But the Rose replied with a shade of sadness in her voice, "Ah, my dear friend, I bloom but for a time: my **petals**⑤ soon wither and fall, and then I die. But your flowers never **fade**⑥, even if they are cut; for they are everlasting."

Greatness carries its own **penalties**⑦.

---

① amaranth /'æməræθ/ *n.* 不凋花
② blossom /'blɔsəm/ *v.* 花开
③ scent /sent/ *n.* 气味，香味
④ universal /ˌjuːni'vɜːsəl/ *a.* 普遍的
⑤ petal /'petl/ *n.* 花瓣
⑥ fade /feid/ *v.* 褪色
⑦ penalty /'penlti/ *n.* 苦恼

一四七　蝎子和瓢虫

　　蝎子与瓢虫交上了朋友，瓢虫成为蝎子的忠实伙伴。一天，瓢虫想过河，可河水又宽又急，很危险，瓢虫游得很吃力，于是，蝎子跟瓢虫说要把她背过河去。他开始对瓢虫有了感情，保证绝不会伤害她。可是，当他们安全地渡过了河，蝎子却由着自己尾巴上的毒针蜇了瓢虫。瓢虫躺在地上，疼痛欲绝，挣扎着问，"……不是说好了吗……为什么呀？"蝎子耸耸身子，悲痛地说，"因为这是我的本性。"

　　无论我们怎样许愿，怎样努力，还是拗不过我们的本性。

CXLVII　The Scorpion and the Ladybug

　　A **Scorpion** ① befriended a **Ladybug** ② who became a loyal companion to him. A time came when she struggled to cross a challenging and dangerous fiver, and so the Scorpion offered to take her to the other side on his back. He had come to care for her and promised he would never harm her. But, safely across the river, he allowed his tail to dip upon her with its **venomous**③ sting. As she lay in greatest pain, she said, "... but, you promised... why?" He **shrugged**④ and said, sadly, "Because it is my Nature."

　　Regardless of our wishes, or even our intent, it is to our Nature alone that we will be faithful.

---

① scorpion /'skɔːpiən/ *n.* 蝎子
② ladybug /'leidibʌg/ *n.* 瓢虫
③ venomous /'venəməs/ *a.* 有毒的
④ shrug /ʃrʌg/ *v.* 耸肩

一四八　海鸥和鸢

海鸥好不容易吞下了一条大鱼，可鱼太大，把他的嗓子胀破了。海鸥躺在岸边，奄奄一息。鸢看见就幸灾乐祸地叫起来："真是活该，哪有天上的飞鸟跑到海里来觅食的?"

各司其职，皆大欢喜。

CXLVIII　The Seagull and the Kite

A **Seagull**[①] having bolted down too large a fish, burst its deep **gullet**[②]-bag and lay down on the shore to die. A Kite saw him and exclaimed: "You richly deserve your fate; for a bird of the air has no business to seek its food from the sea."

Every man should be content to mind his own business.

---

① seagull /'siːgʌl/ *n.* 海鸥
② gullet /'gʌlit/ *n.* 食道

一四九　海边的旅行者

几个人沿着海边行路，爬到一座峭壁的顶上，放眼远眺，看到远处有个物体，以为是艘大船。他们就待在那儿等着，希望看到那艘船驶入港口，可是当那东西被风吹向海岸时，他们发现那充其量不过是只小船，不是大船。当它靠近海岸时，他们看清那只是一大捆木棍。其中一个人对同伴说，"我们白等了，只等到一堆木头。"

我们对生活的期盼往往大于现实。

CXLIX　The Seaside Travelers

Some Travelers, journeying along the seashore, climbed to the summit of a tall **cliff**①, and looking over the sea, saw in the distance what they thought was a large ship. They waited in the hope of seeing it enter the **harbor**②, but as the object on which they looked was driven nearer to shore by the wind, they found that it could at the most be a small boat, and not a ship. When however it reached the beach, they discovered that it was only a large faggot of sticks, and one of them said to his companions, "We have waited for no purpose, for after all there is nothing to see but a load of wood."

Our mere **anticipations**③ of life **outrun**④ its realities.

---

① cliff /klif/ *n.* 悬崖，峭壁
② harbor /'hɑːbə/ *n.* 港
③ anticipation /ænˌtisi'peiʃən/ *n.* 预期，预料
④ outrun /aut'rʌn/ *v.* 超过范围

一五〇 蛇和鹰

鹰从天而降扑向蛇，用爪子抓住蛇，打算把他弄死吃掉。但是蛇的动作更为敏捷，刹那间缠在鹰的身上，鹰和蛇开始了一场生死搏斗。一个乡下人目睹了这一切，赶快上前去帮助鹰，把鹰从蛇的缠绕中解脱出来，让他得以逃生。为了报复，蛇朝乡下人的角杯里吐了些毒液。乡下人因为使劲浑身发热，正要拿起角杯饮水解渴，鹰打落他手中的杯子，水洒了一地。

以德报德。

CL The Serpent and the Eagle

An Eagle **swooped**① down upon a Serpent and seized it in his **talons**② with the intention of carrying it off and **devouring**③ it. But the Serpent was too quick for him and had its **coils**④ round him in a moment; and then there ensued a life-and-death struggle between the two. A countryman, who was a witness of the encounter, came to the assistance of the eagle, and succeeded in freeing him from the Serpent and enabling him to escape. In revenge, the Serpent spat some of his poison into the man's drinking-horn. Heated with his **exertions**⑤, the man was about to **slake**⑥ his thirst with a draught from the horn, when the Eagle knocked it out of his hand, and **spilled**⑦ its contents upon the ground.

One good turn deserves another.

---

① swoop /swuːp/ v. 俯冲
② talon /'tælən/ n. (尤指猛禽的)爪
③ devour /di'vauə/ v. 吞食
④ coil /kɔil/ n. 卷,盘,螺旋
⑤ exertion /ig'zəːʃən/ n. 努力
⑥ slake /sleik/ v. 解渴
⑦ spill /spil/ v. 洒,使……流出

一五一 蛇和锉刀

一条蛇悠来逛去，溜进了一家军械修理店。他在地上蜿蜒滑行，却被放在那里的锉刀扎了一下。蛇勃然大怒，转过头露出毒牙猛地向锉刀咬去，却丝毫不能伤害这个沉重坚硬的铁家伙，不一会儿，他只好悻悻然地咽下怒气，自认倒霉。

攻击无知觉的东西是徒劳无益的。

CLI   The Serpent and the File

A Serpent in the course of its wanderings came into an **armorer**①'s shop. As he **glided**② over the floor he felt his skin pricked by a file lying there. In a rage he turned round upon it and tried to **dart**③ his **fangs**④ into it; but he could do no harm to heavy iron and had soon to give over his **wrath**⑤.

It is useless attacking the **insensible**⑥.

---

① armorer /ɑːmərə/ *n.* 军械士
② glide /glaid/ *v.* 滑动
③ dart /dɑːt/ *v.* 投射
④ fang /fæŋ/ *n.* 尖牙
⑤ wrath /rɔːθ/ *n.* 愤怒
⑥ insensible /in'sensəbl/ *a.* 无感觉的

一五二　母山羊和胡子

母山羊恳求朱庇特让她们也长胡子，得到了批准。公山羊非常恼火，抱怨母山羊跟他们享有同样的尊严。朱庇特安抚地说，"让她们享受虚荣，带着表现男性高贵身份的标识好了，只要她们的力量或勇气不能与你们抗衡。"

能力不如我们的人模仿我们的外表并不重要。

CLII　The She-Goats and Their Beards

The She-Goats having obtained a **beard**① by request to Jupiter, the He-Goats were sorely displeased and made complaint that the females equaled them in dignity. "Allow them," said Jupiter, "to enjoy an empty honor and to assume the **badge**② of your nobler sex, so long as they are not your equals in strength or courage."

It matters little if those who are **inferior**③ to us in merit should be like us in outside appearances.

---

① beard /biəd/ *n.* 胡子
② badge /bædʒ/ *n.* 徽章
③ inferior /in'fiəriə/ *a.* 次等的,较低的

一五三　牧羊人和狗

　　牧羊人把羊赶进圈里过夜，一只狼也和羊一起进去了，牧羊人正要关门时，狗发现了，就开口说，"主人，要是把狼放进圈里，羊怎么能平安呢？"

CLIII　The Shepherd and the Dog

　　A Shepherd **penning**① his sheep in the **fold**② for the night was about to shut up a wolf with them, when his Dog perceiving the wolf said, "Master, how can you expect the sheep to be safe if you admit a wolf into the fold?"

---

① pen /pen/ *v.* 将……关入围栏
② fold /fəuld/ *n.* 羊栏

一五四　牧羊人和海

牧羊人在海边放羊，看见大海风平浪静，不由产生了航海经商的强烈愿望。于是他卖掉羊群，买了一船枣，就出航了。可是海上降下猛烈的暴风雨，船眼看就要沉下去，牧羊人只好抛掉所有的商品，才保全了生命和空船。过了不久，一个人经过海边，说起大海是如何风平浪静。牧羊人打断了他的话说，"它准是又想吃枣了，才显得这么老实。"

CLIV   The Shepherd and the Sea

A Shepherd, keeping watch over his sheep near the shore, saw the Sea very calm and smooth, and longed to make a voyage with a view to **commerce**①. He sold all his flock, **invested**② it in a cargo of dates, and set sail. But a very great **tempest**③ came on, and the ship being in danger of sinking, he threw all his **merchandise**④ overboard, and barely escaped with his life in the empty ship. Not long afterwards when someone passed by and observed the **unruffled**⑤ calm of the Sea, he interrupted him and said, "It is again in want of dates, and therefore looks quiet."

---

① commerce /ˈkɔməs/ n. 商业,贸易
② invest /inˈvest/ v. 投资
③ tempest /ˈtempist/ n. 暴风雨
④ merchandise /ˈmɔːtʃəndaiz/ n. 商品,货物
⑤ unruffle /ˈʌnˈrʌfl/ v. 使平静

一五五　牧童和狼

　　一个男孩在村子附近放羊，一天他突然大喊，"狼来了! 狼来了!"村里人听到了，赶紧跑出来帮助他打狼，看到他们中了圈套，男孩哈哈大笑。男孩把这个把戏玩了三四次，最后狼真的来了。男孩这下真的害怕了，恐惧地放声大叫："求求你们快来帮我啊，狼吃羊了!"可是没人理睬他，更没人来帮助他。于是，狼不慌不忙地捕杀了所有的羊只。

　　说谎的人即使说了真话也没人相信。

CLV   The Shepherd's Boy and the Wolf

A Shepherd-Boy, who watched a flock of sheep near a village, brought out the villagers three or four times by crying out, "Wolf! Wolf!" and when his neighbors came to help him, laughed at them for their pains. The Wolf, however, did truly come at last. The Shepherd-Boy, now really alarmed, shouted in an **agony**① of **terror**②: "Pray, do come and help me; the Wolf is killing the sheep"; but no one paid any **heed**③ to his cries, nor **rendered**④ any assistance. The Wolf, having no cause of fear, at his leisure **lacerated**⑤ or destroyed the whole flock.

There is no believing a **liar**⑥, even when he speaks the truth.

---

① agony /'ægəni/ n. (极度的)痛苦,创痛
② terror /'terə/ n. 恐怖
③ heed /hi:d/ n. 注意,留心
④ render /'rendə/ v. 提供
⑤ lacerate /'læsəreit/ v. 撕裂
⑥ liar /'laiə/ n. 说谎者

一五六　病牡鹿

　　一只生病的牡鹿躺在自己牧场的一角静养，他的很多同伴纷纷前来问候，每只鹿都不客气地吃掉了一点原本为病鹿准备的食物。不久，生病的牡鹿死了，可他并非死于疾病，而是因为缺少食物。

　　交友不良，利少害多。

CLVI　The Sick Stag

A Sick Stag lay down in a quiet corner of its pasture-ground. His companions came in great numbers to inquire after his health, and each one helped himself to a share of the food which had been placed for his use; so that he died, not from his sickness, but from the failure of the means of living.

Evil[①] companions bring more hurt than profit.

---

① evil /'i:vl/ *a.* 坏的，有害的

一五七　牡鹿、狼和羊

牡鹿请羊借给他一些麦子，还说狼会做他的保人。羊担心他们在耍什么花招，就找了个借口说："狼一向是看中了就抢，抢了就跑；而你呢，逃跑的速度远远超过了我。到了还麦子的那天，我怎么能找到你呢？"

黑加黑变不出白色。

CLVII　The Stag, the Wolf, and the Sheep

A Stag asked a Sheep to lend him a measure of wheat, and said that the Wolf would be his **surety**①. The Sheep, fearing some **fraud**② was intended, excused herself, saying, "The Wolf is accustomed to seize what he wants and to run off; and you, too, can quickly **outstrip**③ me in your rapid flight. How then shall I be able to find you, when the day of payment comes?"

Two blacks do not make one white.

---

① surety /'ʃuəti/ n. 担保
② fraud /frɔːd/ n. 欺骗
③ outstrip /aut'strip/ v. 超过

一五八　池边的牡鹿

　　牡鹿酷热难当，来到池边喝水。看着水中的倒影，牡鹿由衷地欣赏自己巨大气派而美丽多姿的角，而对自己纤细瘦弱的腿脚感到很不快。在他思忖的时候，狮子来到池边，弓起身子，扑向牡鹿。牡鹿撒腿就逃，拼命快跑，在开阔平坦的原野上，牡鹿始终可以和狮子拉开距离，可是跑进树林里，牡鹿的角被树枝绊住了，狮子疾跑上去捉住了他。面临不能逃脱的厄运，牡鹿自责不已："我真是太可悲了！竟然欺骗了我自己！能拯救我生命的腿脚，我看不上，引以为荣的角却葬送了我的性命。"

　　真正有价值的东西往往被低估。

CLVIII   The Stag at the Pool

A Stag **overpowered**① by heat came to a spring to drink. Seeing his own shadow reflected in the water, he greatly admired the size and variety of his horns, but felt angry with himself for having such **slender**② and weak feet. While he was thus contemplating himself, a Lion appeared at the pool and **crouched**③ to spring upon him. The Stag immediately took to flight, and exerting his utmost speed, as long as the plain was smooth and open kept himself easily at a safe distance from the Lion. But entering a wood he became **entangled**④ by his horns, and the Lion quickly came up to him and caught him. When too late, he thus reproached himself: "Woe is me! How I have deceived myself! These feet which would have saved me I despised, and I gloried in these **antlers**⑤ which have proved my destruction."

What is most truly valuable is often **underrated**⑥.

---

① overpower /ˌəuvə'pauə/ v. 击败
② slender /'slendə/ a. 细长的,苗条的
③ crouch /'krautʃ/ v. 蹲下
④ entangle /in'tæŋgl/ v. 使……缠绕,纠缠于(某物中)
⑤ antler /'æntlə/ n. 鹿角,茸角
⑥ underrate /ˌʌndə'reit/ v. 低估,估计过低,看轻

一五九　燕子和乌鸦

　　燕子和乌鸦都争说自己的羽毛胜过对方，乌鸦说，"你的羽毛在春天固然很漂亮，但我的羽毛足可为我御寒过冬。"一句话结束了这场争论。

　　不能共患难的朋友不值得交往。

CLIX　The Swallow and the Crow

The Swallow and the Crow had a contention about their plumage. The Crow put an end to the dispute by saying, "Your feathers are all very well in the spring, but mine protect me against the winter."

Fair weather friends are not worth much.

一六〇 小偷和看门狗

一天夜里，小偷闯入一家住宅行窃。他为了不让房子里的看门狗向主人发出警告，特意带了一些肉片来安抚这只狗。正当小偷把肉投给狗时，狗发话了："如果你想用这种方法来堵我的嘴，那可就大错特错了。这种突如其来的仁慈只会使我更加警觉，省得你借着给我意外的好处收买我，谋取你自己的利益，到头来伤害我的主人。"

CLX The Thief and the Housedog

A Thief came in the night to break into a house. He brought with him several **slices**① of meat in order to **pacify**② the Housedog, so that he would not alarm his master by barking. As the Thief threw him the pieces of meat, the Dog said, "If you think to stop my mouth, you will be greatly mistaken. This sudden kindness at your hands will only make me more watchful, lest under these unexpected favors to myself, you have some private ends to accomplish for your own benefit, and for my master's injury."

---

① slice /slais/ *n.* 薄的切片
② pacify /'pæsifai/ *v.* 使……安静

一六一　小偷和公鸡

几个小偷闯进一户人家，除了一只公鸡什么也没找到。他们偷了鸡就赶快逃跑了。一到家他们就要动手宰鸡。公鸡为了保住自己的小命，苦苦央求道："请放过我吧，我对人很有用的。我能在夜里叫醒人们起来工作。""那就更得把你杀了，"小偷们答道，"要是你叫醒你的邻居，我们的生意就全泡汤了！"

想做坏事的恶人恨的就是美德的捍卫者。

CLXI　The Thieves and the Cock

Some Thieves broke into a house and found nothing but a Cock, whom they stole, and got off as fast as they could. Upon arriving at home they prepared to kill the Cock, who thus **pleaded**① for his life: "Pray spare me; I am very serviceable to men. I wake them up in the night to their work." "That is the very reason why we must the more kill you," they replied, "for when you wake your neighbors, you entirely put an end to our business."

The safeguards of virtue are hateful to those with evil intentions.

---

① plead /pliːd/ *v.* 恳求

一六二　口渴的鸽子

一只鸽子渴得唇干舌燥。她看见布告板画着一杯清水，便扇动翅膀，不假思索地猛冲过去，不料重重地撞到板上。鸽子双翅折断，跌在地上，被看热闹的人抓住了。

切勿因头脑发热失去判断力。

CLXII　The Thirsty Pigeon

A Pigeon, oppressed by excessive thirst, saw a **goblet** ① of water painted on a signboard. Not supposing it to be only a picture, she flew towards it with a loud **whir** ② and unwittingly dashed against the signboard, jarring herself terribly. Having broken her wings by the blow, she fell to the ground, and was caught by one of the bystanders.

Zeal should not outrun discretion.

---

① goblet /ˈgɔblit/ *n.* 有脚杯
② whir /wəː/ *v.* 作呼呼声,发飕飕声

一六三　画眉鸟和猎鸟人

画眉鸟正在爱神木上觅食。树上的浆果味道太甜美诱人了，弄得她一直不舍得离开。猎鸟人发现画眉一直待在那棵树上，于是用涂有粘鸟胶的箭射中了她。画眉鸟在临死前嚷道："我真笨，为了一点可口的食物把命都赔上了!"

CLXIII　The Thrush and the Fowler

A Thrush was feeding on a myrtle-tree and did not move from it because its **berries**① were so delicious. A Fowler observed her staying so long in one spot, and having well bird-limed his reeds, caught her. The Thrush, being at the point of death, exclaimed, "O foolish creature that I am! For the sake of a little pleasant food I have **deprived**② myself of my life."

---

① berry /'beri/ *n.* 浆果
② deprive /di'praiv/ *v.* 剥夺

伊索寓言(精选)

一六四 乌龟和鸟

乌龟想搬家。他想请鹰把自己带到新居，答应事成之后给鹰丰厚的报酬。鹰同意了，用爪抓住龟壳，展翅高飞。在途中，他们遇见一只乌鸦。乌鸦悄悄对鹰说："龟肉很好吃啊！""可是龟壳实在太硬。"鹰回答说。"用石头肯定可以轻而易举地砸碎。"乌鸦答道。鹰领会了乌鸦的暗示，突然将龟狠狠地摔在尖利的石块上。然后鹰便与乌鸦开怀地享用了一份乌龟大餐。

绝不要靠着敌人的翅膀飞黄腾达。

CLXIV The Tortoise and the Birds

A Tortoise desired to change its place of residence, so he asked an Eagle to carry him to his new home, promising her a rich reward for her trouble. The Eagle agreed and seizing the Tortoise by the shell with her talons soared **aloft**①. On their way they met a Crow, who said to the Eagle: "Tortoise is good eating." "The shell is too hard," said the Eagle in reply. "The rocks will soon **crack**② the shell," was the Crow's answer; and the Eagle, taking the hint, let fall the Tortoise on a sharp rock, and the two birds made a hearty meal of the Tortoise.

Never soar aloft on an enemy's **pinions**③.

---

① aloft /ə'lɔft/ *ad.* 在高处
② crack /kræk/ *v.* 破裂
③ pinion /'pinjən/ *n.* 鸟翼

一六五　乌龟和鹰

　　一只乌龟懒洋洋地晒着太阳，向海鸟们诉说着自己的不幸，因为从来没谁教她飞行。一只在附近盘旋的鹰听到了乌龟的抱怨，就问乌龟如果把她带到天上，在空中飞翔，能得到什么报酬。"我将给你红海的一切宝物！"乌龟说道。"好吧，那我就教你飞。"说完，鹰抓住乌龟直上云霄。突然鹰把乌龟松开，乌龟一下子掉到高山顶上，龟壳摔得粉碎。乌龟在临死前说道："我真是自作自受。我在地上爬动都这么难，怎么能在云中飞翔呢？"

　　想入非非，往往会自取灭亡。

CLXV   The Tortoise and the Eagle

A Tortoise, lazily **basking**[1] in the sun, complained to the sea-birds of her hard fate, that no one would teach her to fly. An Eagle, **hovering**[2] near, heard her lamentation and demanded what reward she would give him if he would take her aloft and float her in the air. "I will give you," she said, "all the riches of the Red Sea." "I will teach you to fly then," said the Eagle; and taking her up in his talons he carried her almost to the clouds suddenly he let her go, and she fell on a **lofty**[3] mountain, clashing her shell to pieces. The Tortoise exclaimed in the moment of death: "I have deserved my present fate; for what had I to do with wings and clouds, who can with difficulty move about on the earth?"

If men had all they wished, they would be often ruined.

---

① bask /bɑːsk/ v. 晒太阳
② hover /'hɔvə/ v. 盘旋
③ lofty /'lɔfti/ a. 高的

一六六　旅行者和他的狗

　　一个人正要出门旅行，看到他的狗蹲在门边伸懒腰，就厉声地问他，"你怎么还在那儿打哈欠呀？什么都准备好了。就差你啦，快跟我上路吧。"狗摇摇尾巴，回答道，"呵，主人，我早准备好了，正在等您呐。"

　　做事拖拉的人倒常怪动作麻利的同伴误事。

CLXVI　The Traveler and His Dog

　　A Traveler about to set out on a journey saw his Dog stand at the door **stretching**① himself. He asked him sharply: "Why do you stand there gaping? Everything is ready but you, so come with me **instantly**②." The Dog, **wagging**③ his tail, replied: "O, master! I am quite ready; it is you for whom I am waiting."

　　The **loiterer**④ often blames delay on his more active friend.

---

① stretch /stretʃ/ *v.* 伸展
② instantly /ˈinstəntli/ *ad.* 立即
③ wag /ˈwæd/ *v.* 摇摆
④ loiterer /ˈlɔitərə/ *n.* 混日子的人

一六七　两个旅行者和梧桐树

两个旅行者被夏日的太阳烤得筋疲力尽，中午时分，倒在一棵枝干阔展、绿叶婆娑的梧桐树下。他们在浓密的树荫下休息的时候，其中的一个对同伴说，"梧桐树真是无用透顶啊，连果实都不结，对人一点用都没有。"梧桐树打断了他的话说，"你们这些忘恩负义的家伙！享受着我的恩惠，在我的树荫下乘凉，怎么竟敢诋毁我，把我说得一无是处？"

有些人不懂得珍惜上帝的赐福。

CLXVII　The Travelers and the Plane-Tree

Two Travelers, worn out by the heat of the summer's sun, laid themselves down at noon under the widespreading branches of a Plane-Tree. As they rested under its shade, one of the Travelers said to the other, "What a **singularly**① useless tree is the Plane! It bears no fruit, and is not of the least service to man." The Plane-Tree, interrupting him, said, "You ungrateful fellows! Do you, while receiving benefits from me and resting under my shade, dare to describe me as useless, and unprofitable?"

Some men underrate their best blessings.

---

① singularly /'siŋgjuləli/ *ad.* 不可思议地，少见地

一六八 树和斧子

有个人到树林里去，要求树给他一个斧柄。树同意了，给了他一棵小梣树。他刚给斧子安上新柄，就挥动斧子，砍倒很多名贵的参天大树。

一棵老橡树看到他的同伴惨遭荼毒，一切已不可挽回，哀痛不已，惨然地对邻近他的雪松说：“我们第一步就输了全局。如果我们不放弃梣树的生存权利，也许我们还能保持自己的权利，再活几百年呢。”

CLXVIII   The Trees and the Axe

A Man came into a forest and asked the Trees to provide him a handle for his axe. The Trees consented to his request and gave him a young **ash-tree**①. No sooner had the man fitted a new handle to his axe from it, than he began to use it and quickly felled with his strokes the noblest **giants**② of the forest.

An old oak, lamenting when too late the destruction of his companions, said to a neighboring **cedar**③, "The first step has lost us all. If we had not given up the rights of the ash, we might yet have retained our own **privileges**④ and have stood for ages."

---

① ash-tree 梣木
② giant /'dʒaiənt/ *n.* 巨物
③ cedar /'siːdə/ *n.* 西洋杉，香柏
④ privilege /'privilidʒ/ *n.* 权利

一六九　被俘的号兵

　　号兵勇敢地率领士兵前进，被敌人抓获。他对抓他的人大叫道："求求你饶了我，别不分青红皂白就要我的命，我没杀你们一个人。我没有武器，除了这只铜号，身上什么也没带。""正因如此，才要杀掉你。"敌人说，"尽管你自己不参加战斗，你的号角激起所有人去参战。"

CLXIX　The Trumpeter Taken Prisoner

　　A **Trumpeter**①, bravely leading on the soldiers, was captured by the enemy. He cried out to his **captors**②, "Pray spare me, and do not take my life without cause or without inquiry. I have not **slain**③ a single man of your troop. I have no arms, and carry nothing but this one **brass**④ trumpet." "That is the very reason for which you should be put to death," they said, "for, while you do not fight yourself, your trumpet **stirs**⑤ all the others to battle."

---

① trumpeter /'trʌmpitə/ n. 号兵
② captor /'kæptə/ n. 捕捉者，逮捕者
③ slain /slein/ v. 杀害
④ brass /brɑːs/ n. 黄铜
⑤ stir /stəː/ v. 激起

一七〇　树和芦苇

"喂，小家伙，"树对它脚下的芦苇说，"你为什么不学我的样，把根深深地扎入地里，勇敢地在空中昂起头呢?"

"我觉得我这样就挺好的，"芦苇回答道，"也许我不显得那么气派潇洒，但我觉得这样比较安全。"

"安全!"树嗤之以鼻，"谁能把我连根拔起，或让我的脑袋伏在地上?"但是不久树就为它的大话后悔了。因为突然刮起了飓风，树被连根拔出卷到天上，然后砸到地上，成了一段毫无用处的木头。可小芦苇弯下腰，顶着狂风，等风停了，又直起了身子。

平庸无名倒常能保身家性命。

CLXX   The Tree and the Reed

"Well, little one," said a Tree to a **Reed**① that was growing at its foot, "why do you not plant your feet deeply in the ground, and raise your head **boldly**② in the air as I do?"

"I am contented with my lot," said the Reed. "I may not be so grand, but I think I am safer."

"Safe!" **sneered**③ the Tree. "Who shall **pluck**④ me up by the roots or bow my head to the ground?" But it soon had to repent of its boasting, for a **hurricane**⑤ arose which tore it up from its roots, and cast it a useless log on the ground, while the little Reed, bending to the force of the wind, soon stood upright again when the storm had passed over.

Obscurity⑥ often brings safety.

---

① reed /riːd/ *n.* 芦苇
② boldly /'bəuldli/ *ad.* 显眼地；大胆地
③ sneer /sniə/ *v.* 嘲笑
④ pluck /plʌk/ *v.* 猛拉，拔
⑤ hurricane /'hʌrikən/ *n.* 飓风
⑥ obscurity /əb'skjuəriti/ *n.* 身份低微

一七一　受诸神庇护的树

　　根据古代传说，诸神各选了一棵树置于他们的特殊保护之下。朱庇特选中了橡树，维纳斯选了桃金娘树，阿波罗选的是月桂，自然女神希布莉挑了柏树，大力神赫拉克勒斯看上了白杨。智慧女神密涅瓦不知他们为什么都喜欢不结果实的树，就打听他们选择的理由。

　　朱庇特答道，"省得别人以为我们贪图的是结果的荣誉。"可是智慧女神密涅瓦不同意，说，"别人爱说什么说什么，我最喜欢橄榄树，就是因为它能结果。"朱庇特赞许地说，"我的女儿，你的智慧真是名不虚传。徒劳无益，得到的只是虚荣。"

CLXXI   The Trees Under the Protection of the Gods

The Gods, according to an ancient legend, made choice of certain trees to be under their special protection. Jupiter chose the oak, Venus the **myrtle**[①], Apollo the **laurel**[②], Cybele the **pine**[③], and Hercules the **poplar**[④]. Minerva, wondering why they had preferred trees not yielding fruit, inquired the reason for their choice.

Jupiter replied, "It is **lest**[⑤] we should seem to **covet**[⑥] the honor for the fruit." But said Minerva, "Let anyone say what he will, the **olive**[⑦] is more dear to me on account of its fruit." Then said Jupiter, "My daughter, you are rightly called wise; for unless what we do is useful, the glory of it is vain."

① myrtle /ˈməːtl/ *n.*【植】桃金娘科
② laurel /ˈlɔrəl/ *n.* 月桂树
③ pine /pain/ *n.* 松树
④ poplar /ˈpɔplə/ *n.* 白杨,白杨木
⑤ lest /lest/ *conj.* 唯恐,以免
⑥ covet /ˈkʌvit/ *v.* 垂涎,觊觎
⑦ olive /ˈɔliv/ *n.* 橄榄树

一七二　两只袋子

古代传说，每个人降临到这个世界上时脖子上都挂着两个袋子，前面的小袋子装满邻居的过错，后面的大袋子装的是自己的缺点。因此人们往往先看到别人的毛病，对自己的毛病则常常视而不见。

CLXXII　The Two Bags

Every man, according to an ancient legend, is born into the world with two bags **suspended**① from his neck, a small bag in front full of his neighbors' faults, and a large bag behind filled with his own faults. Hence it is that men are quick to see the faults of others, and yet are often blind to their own **failings**②.

---

① suspend /səsˈpend/ v. 悬，挂
② failing /ˈfeiliŋ/ n. 缺点，过失

一七三　两只青蛙

两只青蛙比邻而居，一只住在深水塘里，行踪很少给人看见，另一只住在浅水沟里，横穿一条乡村小路。住在水塘的青蛙警告他的朋友，要他换个地方，还劝他搬来一起住，说深水塘安全得多，食物也很丰富。另一只青蛙拒绝了，说他舍不得离开住惯了的地方。几天之后，一辆载重马车经过水沟，把青蛙压死在了车轮之下。

固执己见，到头来自己遭殃。

CLXXIII　The Two Frogs

Two Frogs were neighbors. One **inhabited**① a deep pond, far removed from public view; the other lived in a **gully**② containing little water, and **traversed**③ by a country road. The Frog that lived in the pond warned his friend to change his residence and entreated him to come and live with him, saying that he would enjoy greater safety from danger and more abundant food. The other refused, saying that he felt it so very hard to leave a place to which he had become accustomed. A few days afterwards a heavy wagon passed through the gully and crushed him to death under its wheels.

A **willful**④ man will have his way to his own hurt.

---

① inhabit /in'hæbit/ *v.* 居住于,栖息
② gully /'gʌli/ *n.* 排水沟
③ traverse /'trævəs/ *v.* 横贯
④ willful /'wilful/ *a.* 任性的

一七四 两个罐子

河上漂着两个罐子，一只是陶罐，另一只是铜罐。陶罐对铜罐说："请千万与我保持距离，不要靠近我，因为只要你轻轻碰我一下，我就会粉身碎骨。再说了，我根本不想跟你靠近。"

实力相当的人才能成密友。

CLXXIV The Two Pots

A river carried down in its stream two Pots, one made of **earthenware**① and the other of brass. The Earthen Pot said to the Brass Pot, "Pray keep at a distance and do not come near me, for if you touch me ever so **slightly**②, I shall be broken in pieces, and besides, I by no means wish to come near you."

Equals make the best friends.

---

① earthenware /ˈɔːθənwɛə/ *n.* 陶器
② slightly /ˈslaitli/ *ad.* 些微地

一七五　两个旅行者和斧子

两个人一起赶路，其中一个人从路边捡起一把斧子说，"我发现了一把斧子。""不要这样说，我的朋友，"另一个人回答道，"不要说'我'，应该说'我们'发现了一把斧子。"他们没走多远，就看见斧子的主人追上来，捡斧子的人说，"我们倒霉了。""不对，"另一个人纠正他说，"还是用你第一次的说法吧，我的朋友；当时你怎么想的，现在还那么想好了。说'我'倒霉了，别说'我们'倒霉了。"

分享好处的人应该分担危险。

CLXXV　The Two Travelers and the Axe

Two men were journeying together. One of them picked up an axe that lay upon the path, and said, "I have found an axe." "Nay, my friend," replied the other, "do not say 'I', but 'we' have found an axe." They had not gone far before they saw the owner of the axe pursuing them, and he who had picked up the axe said, "We are **undone**①." "Nay," replied the other, "keep to your first **mode**② of speech, my friend; what you thought right then, think right now. Say 'I', not 'we' are undone."

He who shares the prize ought to share the danger.

---

① undone /ˈʌnˈdʌn/ a. 已毁灭的，败落的
② mode /məud/ n. 方式

一七六　狐狸和狮子

　　一个明媚和煦的早上，狐狸带着她的孩子们出去散步，路上遇见狮子抱着她的幼儿。"您不就只有这么一个小孩吗，有什么好神气的呀？傲慢的狮夫人。"狐狸揶揄着狮子，"看看我有这么多健康的宝宝。只要您不乏想象力，就不难想到母亲自豪的感觉该有多爽啊。"狮子扫了她一眼，平静地说："不错，看看那好美丽的一窝，谁家的？狐狸家的！我只有一个孩子，可是不要忘记，我的孩儿是狮子。"说完，狮子昂着头走了。

　　质量重于数量。

CLXXVI　The Vixen and the Lioness

　　A Vixen who was taking her babies out for an airing one **balmy**① morning, came across a Lioness, with her cub in arms. "Why such airs, **haughty**② dame, over one **solitary**③ cub?" sneered the Vixen. "Look at my healthy and numerous **litter**④ here, and imagine, if you are able, how a proud mother should feel." The Lioness gave her a **squelching**⑤ look, and lifting up her nose, walked away, saying calmly, "Yes, just look at that beautiful collection. What are they? Foxes! I've only one, but remember, that one is a Lion."

　　Quality is better than quantity.

---

① balmy /ˈbɑːmi/ *a.* 温暖的
② haughty /ˈhɔːti/ *a.* 傲慢的
③ solitary /ˈsɔlitəri/ *a.* 孤独的
④ litter /ˈlitə/ *n.*（猪、狗、猫等多产动物）一胎生下的仔畜
⑤ squelch /skweltʃ/ *v.* 镇压；震慑

一七七 核桃树

路旁的核桃树上结满了果实。过路人为了吃到核桃，用石头和木棍将树枝打断。核桃树哀叹道："我怎么这样不幸啊！我用自己的果实款待过路人，可他们竟然用疼痛来报答我!"

CLXXVII The Walnut-Tree

A **Walnut** ①-Tree standing by the roadside bore an abundant **crop**② of fruit. For the sake of the nuts, the passers-by broke its branches with stones and sticks. The Walnut-Tree **piteously** ③ exclaimed, "O **wretched**④ me! That those whom I cheer with my fruit should repay me with these painful **requitals**⑤! "

---

① walnut /'wɔːlnət/ n. 胡桃
② crop /krɔp/ n. 农作物
③ piteously /'pitiəsli/ ad. 可怜地,凄惨地
④ wretched /'retʃid/ a. 可怜的,不幸的
⑤ requital /ri'kwaitl/ n. 报酬,还礼

一七八　寡妇和她的小女仆

有个寡妇生性爱干净，雇了两个女仆伺候她。寡妇习惯在凌晨鸡叫的时候把仆人叫醒，这样，女仆就得多干许多活。女仆很气愤，决计杀了那只叫早的公鸡。公鸡杀掉了，可是她们却发现，她们的日子反而更难过了，女主人听不到公鸡的打鸣声，半夜就让她们起来去干活。

CLXXVIII　The Widow and Her Little Maidens

A Widow who was fond of cleaning had two little maidens to wait on her. She was in the habit of waking them early in the morning, at **cockcrow** ① . The maidens, **aggravated** ② by such excessive labor, resolved to kill the cock who roused their **mistress** ③ so early. When they had done this, they found that they had only prepared for themselves greater troubles, for their mistress, no longer hearing the hour from the cock, woke them up to their work in the middle of the night.

---

① cockcrow /ˈkɔkkrəu/ *n.* 鸡叫
② aggravate /ˈægrəveit/ *v.* 激怒
③ mistress /ˈmistris/ *n.* 女主人

一七九　寡妇和羊

一个穷寡妇只有一只羊，到了剪毛的季节，她想要羊毛，又不舍得花钱雇人，就自己动手剪。可她不会使用羊毛剪，连羊肉都剪下来了。羊疼得满地打滚，咩咩地哭叫说："你干吗要这样伤害我，女主人？羊血能给羊毛增加多少分量呀？你要是想要我的肉，把屠夫叫来好了，他一刀就会杀了我；要是想要我的毛，还是找剪毛工来吧，他既能剪下羊毛，又不会伤害我。"

最少的开支并非总能获得最大的收益。

CLXXIX　The Widow and the Sheep

A certain poor widow had one solitary Sheep. At **shearing**① time, wishing to take his **fleece**② and to avoid expense, she sheared him herself, but used the **shears**③ so unskillfully that with the fleece she sheared the flesh. The Sheep, **writhing**④ with pain, said, "Why do you hurt me so, Mistress? What weight can my blood add to the wool? If you want my flesh, there is the butcher, who will kill me in an instant; but if you want my fleece and wool, there is the shearer, who will shear and not hurt me."

The least **outlay**⑤ is not always the greatest gain.

---

① shear /ʃiə/ *v.* 修剪，割
② fleece /fliːs/ *n.* 羊毛
③ shears /ʃiə/ *n.* [复]大剪刀
④ writhe /raið/ *v.* (因痛苦而)扭动身体，蠕动
⑤ outlay /'autlei/ *n.* 费用

一八〇　野驴和狮子

野驴和狮子结成联盟，好更容易地捕捉森林中的动物，狮子力气大，可以帮助野驴，野驴跑得快，狮子也可以沾光。他们捉了足够多的动物之后，狮子把猎物分成三份。"我拿第一份，"狮子说，"因为我是林中之王；作为合作的伙伴，我还应拿第二份；至于第三份，除非你甘心放弃，尽快离开逃命，否则就会成为罪孽之源。"

力量就是真理。

CLXXX　The Wild Ass and the Lion

A Wild Ass and a Lion entered into an alliance so that they might capture the beasts of the forest with greater ease. The Lion agreed to assist the Wild Ass with his strength, while the Wild Ass gave the Lion the benefit of his greater speed. When they had taken as many beasts as their necessities required, the Lion undertook to distribute the prey, and for this purpose divided it into three shares. "I will take the first share," he said, "because I am King; and the second share, as a partner with you in the **chase**[①]; and the third share (believe me) will be a source of great evil to you, unless you willingly **resign**[②] it to me, and set off as fast as you can."

Might makes right.

---

① chase /tʃeis/ *n.* 狩猎
② resign /ri'zain/ *v.* 放弃，让出

一八一　野猪和狐狸

野猪站在树下，靠着树干霍霍地磨牙。狐狸经过看见了就问野猪，现在平安无事，既没有猎人也没有猎犬的威胁，为什么要磨牙。野猪回答说："我这样做是未雨绸缪啊，临到用时现磨牙可绝对来不及。"

CLXXXI　The Wild Boar and the Fox

A Wild Boar stood under a tree and **rubbed**① his **tusks**② against the **trunk**③. A Fox passing by asked him why he thus sharpened his teeth when there was no danger threatening from either huntsman or **hound**④. He replied，"I do it **advisedly**⑤; for it would never do to have to sharpen my weapons just at the time I ought to be using them."

---

① rub /rʌb/ v. 擦，搓
② tusk /tʌsk/ n. 獠牙，长牙
③ trunk /trʌŋk/ n. 树干
④ hound /haund/ n. 猎狗
⑤ advisedly /ədˈvaizidli/ ad. 经过考虑地

一八二 狼和鹤

狼的喉咙里卡了一块骨头，于是他出大价钱雇来一只鹤，让他把头伸进自己嘴里，把骨头箍出来。鹤叼出了骨头，向狼讨取说定的工钱。狼狞笑着，磨着牙，恶狠狠地叫起来，"什么工钱？你的脑袋伸到我嘴里，还能平安无事地出来，都是我手下留情，这就足够报答你了。"

为恶人做事可别指望报酬，出力不受伤害就是万幸。

CLXXXII　The Wolf and the Crane

A Wolf who had a bone stuck in his throat hired a Crane, for a large sum, to put her head into his mouth and draw out the bone. When the Crane had **extracted**[①] the bone and demanded the promised payment, the Wolf, **grinning**[②] and grinding his teeth, exclaimed: "Why, you have surely already had a sufficient recompense, in having been permitted to draw out your head in safety from the mouth and jaws of a wolf."

In serving the wicked, expect no reward, and be thankful if you escape injury for your pains.

---

① extract /iks'trækt/ *v.* 提取
② grin /grin/ *v.* 咧嘴而笑

一八三　狼和狐狸

从前狼群里出了一只异常硕大强壮的狼，力量、个头和速度都在别的狼之上，是狼群中的巨无霸，于是群狼一致决定叫他"狮子"。这只狼却不具备与他巨大体形相称的判断力。他以为他们是真心诚意地这么叫他，就离开自己的同类，终日只与狮子厮混。

一只狡猾的老狐狸看到了，就说："希望我永远不会像你那样，因为傲慢自大把自己搞得如此可笑；即便在狼群里你的个头像狮子，在狮子中间，你肯定还是狼。"

CLXXXIII　The Wolf and the Fox

At one time a very large and strong Wolf was born among the wolves, who **exceeded**[1] all his fellow-wolves in strength, size, and **swiftness**[2], so that they unanimously decided to call him "Lion." The Wolf, with a lack of sense **proportioned**[3] to his **enormous**[4] size, thought that they gave him this name in earnest, and, leaving his own race, **consorted**[5] exclusively with the lions.

An old sly Fox, seeing this, said, "May I never make myself so ridiculous as you do in your pride and **self-conceit**[6]; for even though you have the size of a lion among wolves, in a **herd**[7] of lions you are **definitely**[8] a wolf."

---

① exceed /ik'si:d/ v. 超过,胜过　　② swift /swift/ a. 快的,迅速的
③ proportioned /prəu'pɔ:ʃənd/ a. 成比例的,相称的　　④ enormous /i'nɔ:məs/ a. 巨大的,庞大的
⑤ consort /kən'sɔ:t/ v. 陪伴,结交　　⑥ self-conceit /'selfkən'si:t/ n. 自负,自大
⑦ herd /hə:d/ n. 兽群　　⑧ definitely /'definitli/ ad. 肯定地

一八四　狼和马

狼走出一片燕麦田，遇到一匹马，就对他说："快到地里去吧。那里的燕麦长得可好了，我一点没动，全给你留着呢，因为你是我的朋友，我就爱听你津津有味地吃东西的声音。"马回答说："要是燕麦是狼的食品，你绝不会空着肚子只让耳朵享福的。"

恶名在外的人就是做好事也不会得到信任。

CLXXXIV　The Wolf and the Horse

A Wolf coming out of a field of oats met a Horse and thus addressed him: "I would advise you to go into that field. It is full of fine oats, which I have left untouched for you, as you are a friend whom I would love to hear enjoying good eating." The Horse replied, "If oats had been the food of wolves, you would never have **indulged**[1] your ears at the cost of your belly."

Men of evil **reputation**[2], when they perform a good deed, fail to get **credit**[3] for it.

---

[1] indulge /in'dʌldʒ/ *v.* 使沉溺于；使享受
[2] reputation /ˌrepju'teiʃən/ *n.* 名誉，名声
[3] credit /'kredit/ *n.* 信任；赞扬，声望

一八五　狼和看家狗

狼看到獒犬吃得膘肥体壮，脖子上套着沉重的木圈，便问他，是谁把他喂养得这么好，可是又强迫他无论走到哪儿都得驮着那块沉重的木头。"是主人，"獒犬回答道。狼对他说："但愿我的朋友们不会遭此厄运！枷锁的负担足以败坏胃口。"

CLXXXV　The Wolf and the Housedog

A Wolf, meeting a big well-fed **Mastiff**① with a wooden **collar**② about his neck, asked him who it was that fed him so well and yet compelled him to drag that heavy log about wherever he went. "The master," he replied. Then said the Wolf: "May no friend of mine ever be in such a **plight**③; for the weight of this chain is enough to **spoil**④ the **appetite**⑤."

---

① mastiff /'mæstif/ n. 大型猛犬之一种
② collar /'kɔlə/ n. 项圈
③ plight /plait/ n. 情况，(尤指)苦境
④ spoil /spɔil/ v. 破坏
⑤ appetite /'æpitait/ n. 食欲，胃口

一八六　狼和小羊

一只小羊站在屋顶上，看到下面一只狼走过来，便立刻起劲地骂开了。"你这个凶手盗贼，"他叫嚷着，"你跑到诚实的人家来干什么？谁不知道你干尽坏事，你怎么居然还敢露面？"

"你就使劲骂去吧，我的小朋友。"狼说。

明知没危险，正好显勇敢。

CLXXXVI　The Wolf and the Kid

A Kid was **perched**① up on the top of a house, and looking down saw a Wolf passing under him. Immediately he began to **revile**② and attack his enemy. "Murderer and thief," he cried, "what do you here near honest folks' houses? How dare you make an appearance where your **vile**③ deeds are known?"

"Curse away, my young friend," said the Wolf.

It is easy to be brave from a safe distance.

---

① perch /pəːtʃ/ *v.* 位于
② revile /ri'vail/ *v.* 痛斥
③ vile /vail/ *a.* 极坏的

一八七　狼和羊

狼被狗咬得遍体鳞伤，躺在窝里动不了。他肚子空空的，看到羊从他窝前经过，就把羊叫住，请他帮着从旁边的小河里取点水。"因为，"狼说，"要是你能给我打点水，我就有办法为自己找到肉。""想得倒不错，"羊说，"要是我给你带水来，你肯定会把我当肉吃了。"

虚伪的言辞一眼就戳穿。

CLXXXVII　The Wolf and the Sheep

A Wolf, **sorely**① wounded and bitten by dogs, lay sick and **maimed**② in his lair. Being in want of food, he called to a Sheep who was passing, and asked him to fetch some water from a stream flowing close beside him. "For," he said, "if you will bring me drink, I will find means to provide myself with meat." "Yes," said the Sheep, "if I should bring you the **draught**③, you would doubtless make me provide the meat also."

Hypocritical④ speeches are easily seen through.

---

① sorely /'sɔːli/ ad. 剧烈地
② maim /meim/ v. 使残废,使不能工作,使伤残
③ draught /drɑːft/ n. 一份饮料
④ hypocritical /ˌhipəˈkritikəl/ a. 伪善的

一八八　狼和小羊

　　从前，有一只狼在山脚的泉水里舔水喝，突然瞥见一只羊羔在泉水下游的地方喝水。"有晚饭了，"狼暗想，"只要我能想个借口抓住它。"于是他朝小羊喊，"你怎么敢把我喝的水弄脏?"

　　"我没有啊，老爷。"小羊说，"如果您那儿的水浑了，也不可能是我搞的，水是由您那里流到我这儿的。"

　　"就算是这样吧，"狼说，"去年这个时候你为何要骂我?"

　　"那是不可能的，"小羊申辩道，"我才只有六个月大呢。"

　　"我才不管呐，"狼咆哮起来，"不是你就是你爸。"边说边向小羊扑过去，几口把小羊吃得干干净净。小羊在死前喘息着说："暴君是无需借口的。"

CLXXXVIII   The Wolf and the Lamb

Once upon a time a Wolf was **lapping**① at a spring on a hillside, when, looking up, what should he see but a Lamb just beginning to drink a little lower down. "There's my supper," thought he, "if only I can find some excuse to seize it." Then he called out to the Lamb, "How dare you **muddle**② the water from which I am drinking?"

"Nay, master, nay," said **Lambkin**③; "if the water be muddy up there, I cannot be the cause of it, for it runs down from you to me."

"Well, then," said the Wolf, "why did you call me bad names this time last year?"

"That cannot be," said the Lamb; "I am only six months old."

"I don't care," **snarled**④ the Wolf, "if it was not you, it was your father"; and with that he rushed upon the poor little Lamb and ate her all up. But before she died she gasped out: "Any excuse will serve a **tyrant**⑤."

---

① lap /læp/ v. 舔
② muddle /'mʌdl/ v. 把……弄乱,混在一起
③ lambkin /'læmkin/ n. 小羊
④ snarl /snɑ:l/ v. 咆哮
⑤ tyrant /'taiərənt/ n. 暴君

一八九　披着羊皮的狼 （版本一）

从前，有一只狼为了不费力地获取食物，打算把自己伪装起来。他披上羊皮，与羊群一起"吃草"，骗过了牧羊人。晚上他被牧羊人关进羊圈。门关上了，出口也封得严严实实。可是，当晚牧羊人又来到羊圈，打算弄只羊作为第二天的食物。他误把狼当成羊，抓起来一刀结果了狼的性命。

欲害人，反害己。

CLXXXIX　The Wolf in Sheep's Clothing

Once upon a time a Wolf resolved to disguise his appearance in order to secure food more easily. **Encased**[①] in the skin of a sheep, he **pastured**[②] with the flock deceiving the shepherd by his **costume**[③]. In the evening he was shut up by the shepherd in the fold; the gate was closed, and the entrance made thoroughly secure. But the shepherd, returning to the fold during the night to obtain meal for the next day, mistakenly caught up the Wolf instead of a sheep, and killed him instantly.

Harm seek, harm find.

---

① encase /in'keis/ *v.* 将某物置于套、箱等中
② pasture /'pɑːstʃə/ *v.* 吃（草）
③ costume /'kɔstjuːm/ *n.* 服装，剧装

一九〇 披着羊皮的狼 (版本二)

狼发现牧羊人和他的狗极为警觉，很难靠近羊群。有一天，它在野外发现了一只被宰杀了的母羊的皮被扔在了一边，便把它披在自己身上混入羊群。母羊的孩子看了，以为是他妈妈，便跟在狼后面走。狼带着羊羔离开羊群，把小羊吃掉了。狼对羊的诱骗屡屡得逞，过了一段饱享羊肉的好日子。

千万不要被外表所迷惑。

CXC　The Wolf in Sheep's Clothing

A Wolf found great difficulty in getting at the sheep owing to the **vigilance**[①] of the shepherd and his dogs. But one day it found the skin of a sheep that had been **flayed**[②] and thrown aside, so it put it on over its own **pelt**[③] and strolled down among the sheep. The Lamb that belonged to the sheep, whose skin the Wolf was wearing, began to follow the Wolf in the sheep's clothing; so, leading the Lamb a little apart, he soon made a meal off her, and for some time he succeeded in deceiving the sheep, and enjoying hearty meals.

Appearances are deceptive.

---

① vigilance /'vidʒiləns/ *n.* 警戒，警觉心
② flay /flei/ *v.* 剥皮，去皮
③ pelt /pelt/ *n.* 毛皮

一九一 狼、狐狸和猿

狼控告狐狸偷窃，可狐狸死不认账。猿负责对他们的争论进行裁决。双方都振振有词地陈诉了自己的理由。最后猿宣布了审理结果："狼，尽管你说丢了东西，我认为你其实并没丢东西；狐狸，尽管你死不承认，我仍然认为你偷了东西。"

不诚实的人即使做诚实的事，也不会得到信任。

CXCI   The Wolf, the Fox, and the Ape

A Wolf **accused**① a Fox of theft, but the Fox entirely denied the charge. An Ape undertook to **adjudge**② the matter between them. When each had fully stated his case the Ape announced this sentence: "I do not think you, Wolf, ever lost what you claim; and I do believe you, Fox, to have stolen what you so **stoutly**③ deny."

The dishonest, if they act honestly, get no credit.

---

① accuse /əˈkjuːz/ *v.* 控告
② adjudge /əˈdʒʌdʒ/ *v.* 宣判，判决
③ stoutly /ˈstautli/ *ad.* 坚决地

一九二　妇人和她的母鸡

妇人养了一只鸡，每天下一个蛋。她常想怎么样才能一天得两个蛋，而不是一个蛋，最后，为了达到目的，她决定每天给母鸡两份大麦。从那天起，母鸡越长越肥，羽毛也变得油光水滑，却再也不下蛋了。

CXCII　The Woman and Her Hen

A Woman **possessed**① a Hen that gave her an egg every day. She often **pondered**② how she might obtain two eggs daily instead of one, and at last, to gain her purpose, **determined**③ to give the Hen a double **allowance**④ of **barley**⑤. From that day the Hen became fat and **sleek**⑥, and never once laid another egg.

---

① possess /pə'zes/ *v.* 持有
② ponder /'pɔndə/ *v.* 沉思，考虑
③ determine /di'tə:min/ *v.* 决定
④ allowance /ə'lauəns/ *n.* 限额，定量
⑤ barley /'bɑ:li/ *n.* 大麦
⑥ sleek /sli:k/ *a.* (毛发等)光滑的;(喂养得)膘肥体壮的

一九三 年轻的贼和他的母亲

一个年轻人偷东西被当场抓住，为此被判处死刑。他希望被带去处死前见见他妈妈，说几句话，当然，他的要求获得了批准。

看到他妈妈来了，他说："我想和你小声说几句话。"于是他妈妈就把耳朵凑过去，他一口咬下去，几乎把他妈妈的耳朵咬下来。旁边的人吓坏了，问他干吗这么残忍。

"这是为了惩罚她。"他说，"我小时开始小偷小摸，把偷的东西带回家给她。她不但没有骂我、惩罚我，还高兴地说，没人会知道的。就是因为她，我才落到今天这个地步。"

"他说得很对，妇人。"牧师说，"上帝教导说：孩子小时候引导上正路，长大是不会走歪道的。"

CXCIII   The Young Thief and His Mother

A young Man had been caught in a daring act of theft and had been **condemned**[1] to be executed for it. He expressed his desire to see his Mother, and to speak with her before he was led to **execution**[2], and of course this was **granted**[3].

When his Mother came to him he said: "I want to **whisper**[4] to you," and when she brought her ear near him, he nearly bit it off. All the bystanders were **horrified**[5], and asked him what he could mean by such brutal and inhuman conduct.

"It is to punish her," he said. "When I was young I began with stealing little things, and brought them home to Mother. Instead of **rebuking**[6] and punishing me, she laughed and said: It will not be noticed. It is because of her that I am here today."

"He is right, woman," said the Priest; "the Lord hath said: Train up a child in the way he should go; and when he is old he will not depart **therefrom**[7]."

---

① condemn /kən'dem/ *v.* 判刑

② execution /ˌeksi'kjuːʃən/ *n.* 死刑

③ grant /grɑːnt/ *v.* 同意

④ whisper /'hwispə/ *v.* 耳语

⑤ horrify /'hɔrifai/ *v.* 吓,使……战栗,惊骇

⑥ rebuke /ri'bjuːk/ *v.* 斥责

⑦ therefrom /ðɛə'frɔm/ *ad.* 由此